D0342825

OUT FOR BLOOD

MIDDLE SCHOOL BITES

OUT FOR BLOOD

BY
Steven Banks

ILLUSTRATED BY Mark Fearing

HOLIDAY HOUSE • New York

HOLIDAY HOUSE is registered in the U.S. Patent and Trademark Office.

Printed and bound in April 2021 at Toppan Leefung, DongGuan, China.

www.holidayhouse.com

First Edition

1 3 5 7 9 10 8 6 4 2

Library of Congress Cataloging-in-Publication Data

Names: Banks, Steven, author. | Fearing, Mark, illustrator.

Title: Out for blood / by Steven Banks ; illustrated by Mark Fearing.

Description: New York : Holiday House, [2021] | Series: Middle school bites; #3

Audience: Ages 8–12. | Audience: Grades 4–6. | Summary:
Eleven-year-old Tom the Vam-Wolf-Zom is juggling the daily routines of
middle school life while also trying to explore his newly acquired
powers, but Darcourt, the werewolf who bit him, and Tanner Gantt, his
archenemy, are not making it easy.

Identifiers: LCCN 2020035155 | ISBN 9780823446162 (hardcover)

Subjects: CYAC: Middle schools—Fiction. | Schools—Fiction.
Vampires—Fiction. | Werewolves—Fiction. | Zombies—Fiction.
Humorous stories.

Classification: LCC PZ7.B22637 Ou 2021 | DDC [Fic]—dc23

LC record available at https://lccn.loc.gov/2020035155

ISBN 978-0-8234-4616-2 (hardcover)

To Annette,
who helps me enormously
with these books and so many
other things that it would take
another book to list them all.

1.

A Strange Conversation

I was talking to a werewolf.

It was the same werewolf who bit me two and a half months ago, a few hours *after* I'd been bitten by a vampire bat and a few hours *before* a zombie bit me. That all happened the day before middle school started.

I'm probably The Most Unlucky Kid Who Ever Lived.

The world's only Vam-Wolf-Zom.

Now it was Thanksgiving weekend. I was at Gram's house with Mom, Dad, and unfortunately, my big sister, Emma. I almost ate the whole turkey at dinner because I was zombie-starving.

Since it was a full moon, I'd turned into a werewolf, and I decided to go for a run in the woods. I stopped to get a drink from a stream and that's when I saw the werewolf, crouched on the other side. I hadn't seen him since he'd bitten me, but I knew it was him right away. Martha Livingston, the vampire who turned me into a vampire, had told me his name was Darcourt.

He looked like a regular wolf and walked on all fours. (I walk upright on my two legs like a human when I'm a werewolf, which I've only been six times so far.)

Darcourt was gray and white, with very large, very sharp, and very white teeth. He was basically big and terrifying, and he looked like he could rip my throat out.

This was a chance to talk to another werewolf. I had a million questions. But he didn't look like he wanted to talk. He looked like he wanted to leap across the stream and eat me. I wasn't going to wait and find out. I was about to turn into a bat and fly away when he spoke.

"Good evening," he said in a low, gruff, serious voice. He sounded *exactly* like a werewolf that was about to attack.

I got ready to become a bat, and then he said, "I'm just messing with you, wolf! Howzitgoin'?"

He didn't sound like he was going to attack me anymore. But I wasn't sure. Sometimes you meet people and they're nice and friendly, and then later on you find out they're not. Like the first time I met Tanner Gantt, one of The Worst People in the

World. We were in third grade. He pretended to be nice for about five minutes and then he punched me and laughed.

Plus, Martha Livingston had said that Darcourt was dangerous, and if I ever saw him I should run.

"Wait a minute . . . I've seen you before," he said. "About two months ago. You were jogging down the road and I bit you on the ankle. I didn't know you were a kid until I got up close. I usually go for adults. More meat. I just saw you running down that road and I saw *dinner*.

"But then that big truck came by and flashed its high beams in my eyes, honking its horn. I didn't know what was going to happen. Maybe Mister Truck Driver might stop? Maybe he's got some silver bullets? I had to get out of there. So all I got was a bite. But, hey, better I turn you into a werewolf, than eat you, right? Then we wouldn't be hanging out."

Was he ever going to stop talking?

"That whole 'eating people' thing? It's in our DNA. I've been trying to quit, and man, it is crazy hard! I go to the meetings. I do the pledge." He raised his right paw. "I will not eat meat, human or animal. Vegetables can't be beat. I'm not a cannibal! But then . . . nature takes over. I am seriously sorry about turning you into a werewolf. So, what's your name?"

"Tom Marks."

"Yeah? I knew a guy named Howard Marks. Had him over for dinner once. He was delicious. So? Are you out here looking for someone to sink your teeth into? Have a little bite?"

"I don't bite people," I said.

Darcourt looked surprised.

"You don't? Seriously? Okay, I'm not going to judge. There are lots of different kinds of were-wolves."

"Can I ask you some questions?"

"Ask away!"

2.

Top Secret

I sat down at the edge of the stream. "How come you're on all fours, like a real wolf?"

He looked offended. "That's kind of a personal question."

"Oh. . . . Sorry."

He threw back his head and laughed. "I'm pulling your tail! I'm a shape-shifter. Anytime I want to go full-on wolf? Bam! It's showtime. I don't need the full moon. But when Mister Full Moon does come up, I don't have a choice."

"Do you really kill people?"

He thought for a moment and sat down on his haunches. "*Kill* is such a strong word. Do I look like somebody who kills people?"

I wasn't going to lie. "Yeah."

"Do *you*?"

"No. How can I kill people if I don't even bite them?"

"Good point. But you do eat meat? Bacon? Chicken? Nice juicy steak?"

"Well, yeah. But I don't kill the animals."

He smiled. "Somebody does."

I couldn't argue with that.

"You hungry, Tom? I saw some rabbit tracks over there. I *love* fresh rabbit. Tasty as they are cute."

"No, thanks. I just ate half a turkey."

"That's right! It's Thanksgiving. Turkey-lurkey time. Mmmm. I could go for some bird. Still, rabbit's not bad. Did you ever have fresh rabbit?"

"No."

I didn't tell Darcourt that I'd eaten my sister's pet mouse, Terrence, last month. Technically, I didn't *eat* him. I just swallowed him for a little while and then I threw him back up. It was gross. I decided not to do anything like that again.

"Hey listen," said Darcourt. "I've got a proposition for you. My pack is called The Howlers. You want to join up? We have some serious big-time fun."

At first, it sounded like a good idea. I quickly made two lists in my head.

Reasons for Joining a Pack
1. No school (which meant no homework, no tests, no Phys Ed)
2. No more Tanner Gantt
3. Wouldn't have to deal with Emma
4. Could howl whenever I wanted to

5. Nobody would stare at me or ask to take a picture with them

Reasons for Not Joining a Pack
1. I'd miss Zeke.
2. I'd miss Annie (if she ever started talking to me again).
3. No more band (if Annie let me back in).
4. There might be a Tanner Gantt–type werewolf in the pack.
5. I'm only a werewolf twice a month.

"Um. . . . Can I think about it?" I asked.

"Sure!"

"Where's your pack now?"

"They're off doing some top-secret awesome stuff, but I can't talk about it until you join up."

"How many werewolves are there?"

"In our pack? We've got six. In the world? Who knows? They don't count werewolves in the census."

"When'd you become a werewolf?"

Darcourt looked around, like he was making sure no one was nearby. He lowered his voice. "Have you ever heard of . . . The Lycanthrope Project?"

"No."

"Top secret government project in Dallas,

Texas, at an old abandoned prison. They wanted to turn people into werewolves for an elite army of super soldiers. I was the first test subject. I escaped. I've been on the run ever since."

I couldn't wait to tell Zeke. He would think it was the coolest thing *ever*.

"Did they make a werewolf army?"

Darcourt let out a big laugh. "Nah! I made that up! That was a movie I saw. Hey, what's your favorite werewolf movie?"

"The old black-and-white one, *The Wolf Man*, with Lon Chaney Junior."

"You've got good taste, my furry friend. Check out *An American Werewolf in London*."

"So, when *did* you turn into a werewolf?" I asked again. "Who bit you?"

"*That* is a good story. Epic. Love to tell you, but don't have enough time tonight."

I realized he wasn't answering my questions.

"Where do you live?"

"Here, there, and everywhere. I like to keep on the move. Hey, do you like being a werewolf, Tom?"

"I'd rather be a normal kid."

"Yeah, I hear you. It is what it is. You have to embrace your werewolf-self. Own it. Joining a pack would help."

I decided to change the subject. "So, Mr. Darcourt, do you have gatherings of werewolves, like vampires do?"

"How'd you know my name? I didn't tell you." His voice wasn't so friendly anymore.

"Oh . . . Martha Livingston told me."

"You know Martha Livingston? The vampire girl from way back in seventeen seventy something? That is one fierce, smart girl. How do you know Martha?"

"She bit me when she was a bat and turned me into a vampire."

His jaw dropped. "What?! She *bit* you?! You're a vamp?!"

"Yeah."

"Are you kidding me? How come I didn't smell you? I can smell a vamp a mile away!"

"Well, technically, I'm only one-third vamp," I explained. "I'm also a zombie."

Darcourt's blue eyes almost popped out of his head.

"You're crazy. There's no such thing. Now you're pulling *my* tail."

"I'm not. I think I'm the first and only one. I'm a Vam-Wolf-Zom."

"Vam-Woof-*What*?"

"Vam . . . Wolf . . . Zom."

"So, you got bitten by all three biters. I gotta take a sniff."

He leaped over the stream and started sniffing me with his big nose. It was a little rude. I'd never had anybody sniff me like that before. But we're both werewolves, so I guess it happens.

"You've got some serious smells going on. . . . Yeah, I smell the zombie. Not bad. Kind of dead, but sweet and meaty. . . . And the vamp smell. That coppery blood. . . . And the musty wolf smell is right in there too." He stopped sniffing,

thankfully, and backed up to look at me. "Tom, the Vam-Wolf-Zom."

Then I heard footsteps.

Coming toward us.

Both our ears perked up and we each went into a crouched position.

3.

A Stranger in the Woods

I hope it's not hunters," whispered Darcourt. "Watch out for those bad boys."

I'd never thought about hunters. One more thing I had to worry about. Most kids my age just think about school—how you look, who likes you, who doesn't, where you sit in the cafeteria, pimples, and growing pains. I have to worry about those things, plus staying out of the sun, getting blood, eating enough food, silver bullets, wooden stakes . . . and now hunters!

"People hunt wolves?" I asked.

"Well, it's illegal to shoot a wolf unless they're attacking you. Of course, they've got to have silver bullets to take *us* out. But if they do? Sayonara. Adios. Auf Wiedersehen. Adieu."

The footsteps got closer. I sniffed. It was Emma. I could smell the perfume she pours on herself every day. I saw her in the distance, through the trees, but she was too far away to see us.

"Hey! Wolf Boy!" she yelled, with her hands cupped around her mouth.

"What?!" I yelled back.

She stopped walking. "Mom and Dad *forced* me to come out here to get you!"

"Why?"

"Because they are cruel and inhumane parents."

"C'mon, Emma. *Why'd* they send you?"

"They want us to have some stupid family togetherness time and watch some movie called *Never Cry Wolf.*"

Darcourt whispered. "That's a good movie. Very pro-wolf."

"I'll be back in a while, Emma!" I yelled. "I gotta do some stuff!"

"What kind of stuff? Wait. Never mind. I don't want to know. I'm sure it's disgusting!"

Emma walked away.

"That's my sister."

"She looks like a nice girl."

I was about to tell him that Emma was the opposite of nice when he said, "Listen, I'll walk back with you and then I've gotta get some food in my belly."

We headed back through the woods to Gram's.

"Hey, Tom, did Martha Livingston ever tell you about an old book, about how to be a vampire? I forget the title."

"*A Vampiric Education* by Eustace Tibbitt? Yeah. She lent me her copy."

His eyes got wide for a second. Then he smiled. A wolf smiling at you is sort of creepy. *Am I creepy when I smile, when I'm a werewolf?* I'll have to ask Zeke.

"Has it taught you how to do vampire stuff?"

"Yeah, I'm trying to transform into smoke. I also

want to get better at hypnotizing people. It's hard if the person doesn't want to be hypnotized."

We jumped over a fallen log.

"Where do you keep the book?" he asked, when we landed on the other side.

The book was in my room, at Gram's, in a secret pocket of my backpack. I'd put another book cover on it: *Danny the Detective.* Emma gave me that book for my birthday last year. She got it out of one of those Little Free Library boxes that people have in front of their houses, so it didn't cost her anything.

Emma always gives me horrible gifts. *Danny the Detective* is a really bad book. Danny is the worst detective ever. I figured out who stole his bike by the second chapter. He missed every clue. My twelfth birthday is coming up on January sixteenth. I wonder what stupid thing Emma will get me this time.

Anyway, I figured it was okay to show the book to Darcourt. He wasn't a vampire. He wouldn't be able to learn how to do any of things. Or would he?

Then, I remembered that when Martha Livingston gave me the book, she'd said, "This was a gift from my instructor, Lovick Zabrecky. Only one hundred copies were printed. If it fell into other hands, I would be *greatly* displeased. It is quite valuable. Do *not* sell it on eBay."

I told Darcourt I hadn't brought the book with me to Gram's house, that I'd left it back home.

"Too bad," he said. "I'd like to check it out. Do you keep it somewhere safe?"

"Yeah. I keep it under my bed, hidden in my baseball mitt."

I would seriously regret telling him that.

4.

Talk to the Animals

Darcourt and I were getting close to Gram's house.

"Hey, Tom, let's keep our little encounter on the down low. Swear, by the blood of the wolf, you won't tell a soul about me?"

"Sure." I raised my paw. "I swear, by the blood of the wolf, I won't tell a soul."

Martha Livingston had also made me swear not to tell anyone about her, but Zeke figured it out. Then, on Halloween she hypnotized him so he wouldn't remember. But Darcourt already knew about Martha, so I figured it was okay that I told him.

"Are there any books about how to do werewolf stuff?" I asked.

"A few. . . . One from the eighteen hundreds is called *The True Story of Sir Edgar Spencer, the Man-Wolf (As Told by His Butler, Before He Was Eaten)*. Another one, *The Big Book of Werewolfing*, is not bad, but it's not good either. *Oh, No! I'm a Werewolf! Now What?* is total junk. The best way to learn werewolf skills is from a real live werewolf. If you join The Howlers, you'll learn a lot."

That was another good reason to join a pack. When we trotted over the hill to Gram's, her neighbor's dog, Stuart, started barking his head off.

Darcourt stopped. "Hey, that dog could be my twin. Brother from another mother."

He barked at Stuart, who then barked back at him.

"Are you talking to him?" I asked.

"Yep."

"You can talk to dogs?"

"Some. He's got a heavy accent, so he's a little hard to understand."

"What'd you say to him?"

"I said, 'Hello. I mean no harm. This is your territory. Respect.'"

"And what'd he say?"

"I *think* he said, 'I have to poop soon and will be embarrassed if you watch.'"

"Can you teach me how to talk to dogs?"

"Yeah . . ."

"Excellent!" I sounded like Zeke.

". . . if we had two weeks for classes." Darcourt stopped walking. "Hey, I'd better not get any closer. Wouldn't want to freak out the fam. Big ol' wolf coming toward the house. 'Hey, Gram, it's Little Red Riding Hood time!' Grams aren't too fond of Big Bad Wolves. . . . So, don't forget my offer about joining The Howlers. Good thing to be part of a pack, hang with your werewolf brothers and sisters, have a posse."

"I won't," I said.

"Maybe I'll come see you sometime. Check out that book. Stay cool, Tom. Stay wolf."

He trotted back into the woods and disappeared. It wouldn't be the last time I'd see him.

5.

Cranberry Sauce

The next Monday, at home, I put on my long-sleeved shirt, sunglasses, hat, and sunscreen and went to the bus stop.

I needed to see if Annie was still mad at me. She thought I'd been spying on her when I'd turned into a bat and flew outside her bedroom window. She even kicked me out of our band. I kept trying to explain, but every time she'd either walk away or talk to someone else like I wasn't there. I even wrote her notes, but she just threw them away without reading.

Capri was also mad at me because I'd said her voice wasn't that good and she should stick to piano. Honesty is not always the best policy.

Zeke was late and ran up just as I was getting on the bus.

"Hey, T-Man! How was your Thanksgiving?"

I really wanted to tell him about Darcourt, but I had sworn I wouldn't.

"It was . . . okay," I said. "How was yours?"

"Excellent! You're not gonna believe this. I finally tried cranberry sauce. I love it! Why didn't anybody tell me it was so awesome? I had some for breakfast on my toast."

When we got on the bus, Annie and Capri were sitting next to each other. Annie was reading a book, as usual. It was called *Poems of Emily Dickinson.*

"Hey, Annie. Hey, Capri," said Zeke.

"Hi, Zeke," said Capri. Then she gave me a dirty look.

Annie looked up from her book and smiled. At Zeke. Not me.

"Don't forget about band practice tomorrow, Zeke."

"Hey, Annie," I said.

Her smile disappeared and she went back to reading her book. I sat down behind her and leaned forward.

"Is that a good book?"

She ignored me, turned the page, and kept reading. I leaned back in my seat. What if Annie never talked to me again for the rest of my life? I had a plan called *The Girlfriend Plan*. I was going to ask Annie to be my girlfriend when we got to high school. If she never talked to me again, it would be hard to do that.

o o o

Tanner Gantt got on the bus. He didn't call me Freak Face or Monster Boy like he usually does. He didn't punch anybody or make fun of anyone or knock books out of their hands. Instead, he slumped down in the first empty seat and looked out the window. He must have been having a bad day too.

Everybody was acting different. Except Zeke.

"T-Man, if this bus could fly, where would you want it to go? I'd want it to go to a cranberry field."

I shrugged. I was trying to figure out a way to get Annie to talk to me. I wanted to get back in the band and be friends again.

Luckily, I was about to get a chance to make that happen.

6.

Crime and Punishment

Mr. Kessler was the only teacher who assigned us homework over Thanksgiving vacation, which was totally unfair. You shouldn't have to do any homework when you're on vacation.

I looked up "vacation" in the dictionary. It said, "An extended period of leisure and recreation." It didn't say anything about writing short stories.

I didn't write mine until the night we got back from Gram's.

THE DEADLY SHORT STORY
by Tom Marks

Tim Martin sadly sat at his desk. He
was on vacation, but he had to write a
story for one of his classes. Tim stayed
up all night writing the story, because he
wanted it to be good, and fell asleep at his
desk. His window blew open and it started
raining. Tim got a cold, the flu, and
pneumonia.

The next day, he handed the story in,
and then he collapsed and died, right in
the classroom. They arrested his teacher
and he went to prison. They renamed the
school The Tim Martin Middle School.
They put up a life-sized statue of Tim in
the front of the school sitting at his desk
writing the story, with a plaque that said:
"He Died Because He Had to Do
Homework During Vacation."

Every day, kids would cry as they
walked past the statue, remembering how
awesome Tim was and how much they
missed him. Some put flowers on the
statue and lit candles and left letters to

Tim and poems about him. The whole school wore T-shirts with Tim's picture on them.

A law was passed that made it illegal for a teacher to assign homework over any vacation. It was called *The Tim Martin Was Right Law*. They made a movie about Tim's life and it won the Oscar for Best Picture and made a billion dollars.

HE DIED
BECAUSE HE
HAD TO DO
HOMEWORK
DURING
VACATION.

When we got to class, Mr. Kessler said we had to read our stories out loud. I read mine and a lot of people laughed. I thought Mr. Kessler would get mad, but he didn't.

"Very amusing story, Mr. Marks."

Then, Annie got up to read hers.

"*The Bird Who Was Not a Bird on the Windowsill*, written by Annie Delapeña Barstow."

I didn't like the sound of that.

"Anita Fresno was sitting on her bed, playing her guitar, when she looked out the window and saw a bird on the windowsill. It was staring at her. She looked closer. It wasn't a real bird. It was a boy at her school, named Terry Sparks, who had magical powers. He was spying on her, invading her private space, looking at her without her permission."

Annie looked up from her paper, gave me a dirty look, and went on reading.

"Anita stood up and shouted at the bird, 'Hey! Get out of here, _____!'"

Then she said a word you're not allowed to use at school. Tanner Gantt says it. So does my dad when he gets mad.

"Annie!" said Mr. Kessler. "You can't say that word in class."

"Why not?"

"It is not appropriate."

"But it's what the character would say."

"That doesn't matter."

"Everybody says it," said Annie.

Maren Nesmith raised her hand. "I have *never* said that word in my whole, entire life and I never will."

That was probably true.

"I bet *you've* said that word, Mr. Kessler," said Annie.

"This isn't about me, Annie. You can't use that word in school."

"That's censorship."

"It is not censorship."

"Yes, it is!" Annie can get mad really fast.

"Calm down," said Mr. Kessler.

"I *am* calm!"

She wasn't calm. People who say 'I *am* calm' never are.

"It is an offensive word," said Mr. Kessler.

Annie looked out at the class. "Was anybody offended by that word?"

Maren Nesmith was the only person who raised her hand.

Annie said, "The character would say _____. It's just a word. Writers have rights. If I want to say _____ in a story, I should be able to say _____!"

Now she'd said the illegal word four times.

"Okay, Ms. Barstow," said Mr. Kessler. "You just got yourself lunch detention."

Annie stormed back to her desk, sat down, and crossed her arms. She had tears in her eyes. But they were "mad tears," not "sad tears." There's a big difference.

"You have to sit at The Table of Shame," whispered Maren Nesmith.

Annie whispered an illegal word to Maren.

7.

Troublemaker

The Table of Shame was a table in the corner of the cafeteria. People who got in trouble had to sit there facing the wall and couldn't talk during lunch. Tanner Gantt had already sat there about six times this year. None of the teachers called it The Table of Shame, only kids did.

Emma had told me about it over the summer. I thought she was lying, but she wasn't. That's the trouble with Emma: sometimes she tells the truth. It's very confusing. She also said that they let kids throw food at you when you are sitting there, which is not true. See what I mean?

I was secretly glad that Annie got in trouble, because it gave me a great idea. If I could figure out a way to get lunch detention, I'd have to sit at The Table of Shame with Annie. I could talk to her and she'd *have* to listen to me.

It wouldn't be easy. I'd have to be careful not to do something that was too bad, like pretend to bite somebody, or I'd get suspended. I made a plan on my way to second period.

GET IN **TROUBLE** AND GET **LUNCH DETENTION** PLAN

☐ Talk in class.

☐ Leave class without a hall pass.

☐ Cut in the snack line.

☐ Cause a disturbance in class.

ATTEMPT #1

During Science, I asked Mr. Prady for a hall pass to go to the restroom. He gave it to me and I walked down the hall, but no one was around. I had to get somebody to see me so I'd get in trouble. I started to whistle, and Principal Gonzales came out of his office. Perfect.

"Hi, Tom," he said.

I froze and looked as guilty as I could.

"Oh. . . . Um. . . . Hi, Principal Gonzales," I said nervously.

"Everything okay?" he asked.

"Um. . . . Yeah . . . I guess," I said.

Now it was time for him to do his job and ask me for my hall pass. But he didn't.

"Good. Have a nice day." He walked off.

"Wait!" I yelled.

He turned around.

"I don't have a hall pass. I forgot to get one. I guess you'll have to give me lunch detention."

He smiled. "I suppose I can let it go this time. But just this once. We all make mistakes."

He walked off whistling.

ATTEMPT #2

At snack time, I cut in front of a long line of

people in the cafeteria and went right to the window ahead of everybody.

"I'll have a bacon-and-egg burrito," I said to Snack Lady.

"Hey! No cuts, Marks!" said Brett Loudermilk, who I've seen take cuts before.

"Back of the line!" said Duke Spencer.

"You'd better give me lunch detention," I said to Snack Lady.

She shook her head. "No way. You're the you-know-what. We don't want you getting too hungry and eating anybody."

"I'm not going to eat anybody," I said for the millionth time.

She handed me the burrito and said, "Not now you aren't."

I ate with Zeke and told him my plan.

"I know what you can do, T-Man!" he said. "Kidnap Principal Gonzales! Or go to the library and yell! Or turn into a bat and fly around and poop on a teacher's head!"

"No! Ew. That is disgusting. Besides, I don't want people to know I can turn into a bat yet."

"When are you gonna show people you can do that?"

"I don't know. It's gotta be the right time."

Zeke, Annie, Abel, Dog Hots, Capri, and Emma were the only people who knew I could turn into a bat and fly. I made them swear not to tell anybody. So far, they hadn't.

Abel, my locker partner, walked up wearing his usual suit and tie and opened his briefcase. He took out some little oval cookies.

"I have some homemade madeleines, if anyone cares to partake?"

Zeke and I each took one. They were delicious. Abel should open a bakery. I told him my problem. He crossed his arms and titled his head to the side.

"I would suggest a minor infraction in class, causing a suitable disturbance. Perhaps rough-housing of some sort: simulated fisticuffs, Greco-Roman wrestling, or some such shenanigans?"

"Excellent!" said Zeke. "Let's pretend we're mad at each other, T-Man, and get in a fight."

"Uh . . . okay," I agreed.

I'm always a little nervous when we do one of Zeke's plans.

ATTEMPT #3

In third-period History, Zeke stood up at his desk and said, "I don't like you, Tom Marks! I've *never* liked you!"

This made absolutely no sense. Everybody knows Zeke and I are best friends.

"You jerk!" he went on. "I'm going to beat you up! Let's fight!"

Zeke is not a good actor. People laughed. We started to wrestle, but Zeke is super ticklish, so he started giggling. It didn't look like we were fighting, it looked like we were having fun.

"What on earth are you boys doing?" asked Mrs. Troller, with a smile on her face.

"We're Greco-Roman wrestling!" said Zeke, laughing.

"Why?"

"To get in trouble," said Zeke, who tells the truth at the oddest moments.

"Okay, settle down," said Mrs. Troller, separating us. "Let's talk about the history of wrestling. Did anyone know that Abraham Lincoln was a champion wrestler?"

She turned it into a history lesson.

I didn't get lunch detention.

Lunch was only two periods away. I was getting desperate. I had to get some expert advice, and there was only one person to ask. Why hadn't I thought of him sooner?

○ ○ ○

Tanner Gantt had just slammed his locker shut when I walked up.

"Hey," I said.

"What do you want, Freak Boy?"

"What's the best way to get lunch detention?"

He looked confused. "Why do you want to know that?"

I shrugged. "Just curious."

"Are you trying to get me in trouble?" he asked, suspiciously.

"No."

"I bet you are!"

"I'm not!"

He got in my face. "Are you wearing a wire?"

Now I was confused. "What?"

"You're recording this, aren't you? And then you're gonna play it for Principal Gonzales."

He walked away.

Tanner Gantt was no help at all.

ATTEMPT #4

In Math class, I decided to get Ms. Heckroth mad at me. That wouldn't be very hard. She's always mad. She was standing at the front of the room, looking even more stern than usual. This was going to be easy.

"Today we will be doing long division and I want you—"

"Why are we learning how to do this, Ms. Heckroth?"

She gets really mad when kids don't raise their hands.

She slowly turned to look at me and narrowed her eyes. "*Excuse me*, Mr. Marks? We raise our hands before we speak and we do not interrupt when someone is—"

"Sorry, I didn't mean to," I said, interrupting her again. "But why are we doing this? Do we really need to know how to do long division?"

"*What?*"

"Will we ever use it in real life?"

"You most certainly will."

"But couldn't we just use the calculator on our phone or look it up on the Internet? We'd only need to know how to do it if we're going to be a math teacher." I turned around to the class. "Does anyone want to be a math teacher?"

Nobody raised their hand.

Ms. Heckroth looked sort of sad. I felt bad, so I stopped talking.

I didn't get lunch detention.

I had to get in trouble during the next class.

8.

The Last Attempt

I went to Art class. Lunch was next period. I was running out of time. I tried to bother Capri by throwing little pieces of paper at her. She started laughing, drew hearts on the paper, and threw them back at me. I guess she wasn't mad at me anymore.

We were drawing a still life of an apple, a bottle, and a hat on top of some books. I'm The Second-Worst Artist in the World, next to Emma. My drawing looked like a giant hamburger attacking New York City. I decided to start a disturbance.

I started humming.

"Mr. Marks, what are you doing?" asked Mr. Baker.

"Humming."

"Why?"

"I like to have music when I'm drawing. It helps me create."

He nodded his head. "You know, that's a good idea. I'll put on some music while we draw."

Why was it so hard to get in trouble?! I added a naked person to the picture I was drawing and held it up.

"Mr. Baker? What do you think of this?"

He scratched his chin and said, "Is that an elephant dancing on top of the Empire State Building?"

I sighed. "No."

I needed to step up my game. I drew a picture of Mr. Baker with a super-long nose and tiny ears, and made him even balder and shorter than he really is.

"This is quite interesting," he said, holding it up so everybody could see. "This style of art is called 'caricature.' Physical features are exaggerated for comical effect. I don't know who Tom is doing a caricature of, but it is quite good."

I looked at the clock. I had five minutes left. While I was trying to think of something, it happened. Without thinking or trying. Completely naturally.

I burped.

"Ew! Gross! It was Tom Marks!" said Maren Nesmith, The Queen of Tattle-Tells.

My uncle Vince had taught me how to burp on command when I was four years old. That was one of the reasons he was my favorite uncle. I sucked in some air and let out another one.

"*Burrrrrrp.*"

"That's enough, Tom," said Mr. Baker.

"*Burrrrrp.*"

"Are you all right, Tom?"

I nodded.

"*Burrrrrp.*"

"Do you need to go to the nurse?"

"No, Mr. Baker. I just like to—*Burrrrrrp.*"

"Okay. No more, Tom. I'm serious."

"*Burrrrrrrp.*"

"Mr. Marks, do you *want* to get lunch detention?"

Yes! Yes! I do! Please! Give it to me!

Mr. Baker continued, "One more outburst and you will spend your lunch in silence."

I let out the longest, loudest, grossest, biggest, most disgusting burp in the history of the world.

"*BURRRRRRRRRRRRRP!*"

"All right, Mister. You have Silent Lunch Detention."

9.

The Table of Shame

There were three Tables of Shame in the cafeteria. One for each grade. Annie was the only person sitting at the sixth-grade table.

Perfect.

The other tables had seventh and eighth graders who looked like they'd been there before.

"Welcome, Table of Shamers. I am your Silent Detention Guard, Kenneth Liversidge," said a tall eighth grader with the blondest hair I have ever seen. "Joining our repeat offenders today, we have two first timers: Mr. Marks and Ms. Barstow. The rules are simple: Eat your lunch, face the wall, and do not talk. Otherwise, you will be here tomorrow. I'll be watching you."

I wouldn't want to watch kids eat lunch and stare at a brick wall for half an hour. You could tell Liversidge liked doing it. I bet he wanted to be a prison guard when he grew up.

I sat down at the table, about four feet away from Annie. She was eating an avocado sandwich and writing on a notepad.

I started eating my chicken-turkey-salami-roast-beef sandwich. Mom and I had discovered that those really filled me up and I wouldn't be zombie-starving until I got home from school.

I glanced over to see what Annie was writing.

"Dear Superintendent of Schools,
The Table of Shame, also known as Silent Lunch Detention, is unconstitutional and a form of cruel and unusual punishment. It should be outlawed."

Out of the corner of my eye, I could see Liversidge watching us. I had to talk to Annie without letting him hear me or see me doing it, but I wasn't worried.

For once, I was glad that Emma was my sister. Three years ago she'd wanted to be a ventriloquist. She saw this girl doing ventriloquism on a TV talent show called *Show Us What You Got!*, and the girl won a bunch of money. Emma got a book on ventriloquism from the library, read the first page, and gave up—like she always does. But I read the book, and now it was going to pay off. I could talk to Annie, and Liversidge wouldn't see my lips moving.

"Annie?" I whispered, barely opening my mouth and not moving my lips. "Just listen to me."

And that's when I heard Principal Gonzales's voice.

"We have one more person joining you, Mr. Liversidge."

I looked over. He was bringing Tanner Gantt toward us. The odds of him getting lunch detention were always pretty high, but why did he have to get it today?

"Welcome back, Mr. Gantt," said Liversidge. "You know the drill."

I couldn't talk to Annie about wanting to be

friends again and getting back in the band with The Worst Person in the World listening.

Tanner Gantt sat down hard and the table shook a little. He was on my left side and Annie was on my right. For his lunch he had three cold hot dogs with no buns, a bag of Sammy's Super Salty chips, and four chocolate chip cookies. I bet he made his own lunch.

I decided that I still had to talk to Annie, since I'd worked so hard to get to The Table of Shame.

"Annie?" I said, using my best ventriloquist technique.

She was chewing and staring at the wall. Tanner Gantt turned his head slightly toward me. I had to choose my words carefully, so he wouldn't know what I was talking about.

"Okay. You don't have to talk to me, but please listen. I'm really, really, really sorry I did that thing I did, that you got mad at me for. You were right. I shouldn't have done it. I just wanted to show you that *thing* I could do, because I thought you'd think it was awesome."

I glanced over at Tanner Gantt. He looked confused. Good.

"Anyway, I'll never do it again. I promise. I want to be back in the you-know-what. But, mostly, I hope you'll talk to me and we can be friends again."

That was the hardest part to say with Tanner Gantt sitting there.

Annie sat for a moment, staring at the brick wall, and then she started writing on her pad again.

Had she listened to me? Had I succeeded? Had I failed? Had Tanner Gantt heard enough to make fun of me for life?

Annie turned her pad toward me. I looked down and read what she'd written:

"Apology accepted. Band practice tomorrow. My house. Three thirty. Don't be late."

Tanner Gantt tried to lean over and see what she wrote, but Annie covered it with her hand.

"Eyes at the wall, Mr. Gantt!" said Liversidge.

Eventually the bell rang and lunch was over.

"You're free to go, Shamers," said Liversidge. "I hope you've learned your lesson today. However, if you return, I'll be right here . . . waiting for you."

10.

Practice Makes Perfect

That night, I decided to practice transforming into smoke. Martha Livingston had shown me how she did it. She could go through tiny cracks under doors or windows or just disappear in a puff of smoke, like a magic trick. It looked easy to do.

But it wasn't.

I took out *A Vampiric Education* by Eustace Tibbitt. The book was so old, and the pages were so thin, I had to be careful turning them so they didn't tear. The first page said:

This book is dedicated to my precious Leonora. My love. My life. My blood. My first vampire who taught me everything.

Eustace Tibbitt

Underneath that, he had signed his name in faded red ink. Or was it blood?

I turned the page and noticed something I hadn't before. Two pages were stuck together. Slowly, I peeled them apart. Someone *else* had written in the book. It was in that old-fashioned cursive writing that I am so glad they don't make us do in school anymore.

To my dearest Martha Livingston,
I hope this book serves you well, as it has I.
Yours forever, and ever and ever,
Lovick Zabrecky
March 13th, 1776
P.S. If you lose this, sell it, or lend it to anyone, I
shall make it my sole purpose in life to hunt you down.
When I find you, it will be an unpleasant experience.

Martha Livingston must have felt it was okay to lend it to me because she said Lovick Zabrecky hadn't been seen for a hundred years. He had to be dead. Still, I was glad I hadn't let Darcourt see the book that night. If he ever showed up again, I'd have to figure out an excuse.

I decided to take a break from trying to turn to smoke and look up *A Vampiric Education* on the Internet.

"A Vampiric Education *by Eustace Tibbitt. An instructional book for vampires, published in 1654. Only two known copies remain. One is at the Smithsonian Institute in Washington, D.C. The other copy, which was originally owned by Bram Stoker (1847–1912), the author of* Dracula, *was bought at auction by the horror writer Stephen*

King. *That copy was stolen from Mr. King's home and has never been found. The reclusive billionaire, Geoffrey Bucklezerg Kane, collector of rare historical items, has a standing offer of one million dollars for the book.* "

The book under my bed, in my old baseball glove, is worth *a million dollars?*

I have to admit, for a second I thought about selling it. Then, I realized if Martha Livingston found out, she'd probably kill me.

The last time I saw her was on Halloween. She tried to suck Tanner Gantt's blood, but I stopped her. Capri and Annie met her and thought she was just a girl dressed up as a vampire. It was totally awkward, and later, Martha teased me about them being my girlfriends. Then, Zeke showed up and she hypnotized him so he wouldn't remember meeting her. While he was hypnotized, I asked her to make him stop doing jumping jacks when he got excited. He hasn't done a single one since.

I wondered when I'd see Martha again. I wanted to tell her about Darcourt. Or I would see Darcourt first?

11.

The Reunion

We had band practice at Annie's house the next day after school.

"We still don't have a name, you guys," complained Capri. "We need a name!"

"We need a bass player," said Dog Hots, setting up his drums.

"We need to do a show," said Zeke, eating cranberry sauce out of a little plastic container he'd brought, along with his banjo.

Abel looked up from tuning his guitar. "Our current repertoire is somewhat sparse. If our

aspirations are to eventually do a live performance, I venture to say we need more material."

"I need to write some more songs," said Annie.

"I need more food," I said, grabbing one of Annie's mom's homemade empanadas. I have to admit, the food was one of the things I missed most about not being in the band.

Capri sat down at the piano. "Annie, let's play Tom that song you wrote, the one we've been practicing."

"You mean 'Spying'?" said Dog Hots.

Annie shook her head. "Uh, no, let's do something else."

"But it's an excellent song!" said Zeke, his mouth full of cranberry sauce.

Personally, I didn't think I wanted to hear "Spying."

"I wrote a new one," said Annie. "It's called "Table of Shame.'"

Abel smiled. "Write what you know."

We actually had a pretty good practice. We worked on three songs, Zeke learned three more chords on the banjo (now he knows five), Capri's voice has gotten better since she took some YouTube lessons, and I ate six empanadas.

I was glad to be back in The Band with No Name.

○ ○ ○

That night, I did more smoke-transforming practice. Still no luck. Why was it so hard? I couldn't concentrate, so I went through the rest of the book. There were plenty of chapters with other skills to learn, and information about being a vampire. Some were interesting and some weren't:

Chapter Three: "How to Hypnotize People and Bend Them to Your Will"
I'd already hypnotized Zeke, but I wanted to get better so I could hypnotize other people with stronger wills.
Chapter Five: "The Sun Is Your Mortal Enemy"
Duh.
Chapter Eight: "Turning Others into Vampires"
I definitely didn't want to do that.
Chapter Nine: "The Art of Sleeping in a Coffin"
I skipped that chapter.
Chapter Thirteen: "Transform to a Wolf at Will"

So far, I only turned into a werewolf when the moon was full. Did I want to do it any other time? Maybe. I had a deep, rough, rock-and-roll voice when I was a werewolf. If I learned how to transform, I'd have a great voice any night our band played. Darcourt could teach me, but I'd have to join his pack. Was it worth it?

Chapter Fourteen: "Transform to a Rat"

Why would anyone ever want to be a rat?

Chapter Eighteen: "How to Trick a Werewolf"

This could be helpful in case Darcourt showed up again. It said you should hypnotize or outwit them. Darcourt seemed pretty smart and strong willed. It wouldn't be easy.

Chapter Nineteen: "Befriending a Ghoul"

"Ghoul" is what they called zombies way back in the 1700s. If I ever found the zombie that bit me, this chapter might be useful.

Chapter Twenty: "The Vampire Art of Romance"

That was a weird one.

For now, I decided to concentrate on transforming into smoke. I practiced for an hour and still couldn't do it. I really wished Martha would come back and give me a lesson.

But one of my other Vam-Wolf-Zom skills was about to be put to good use.

12.

The Scene of the Crime

Your next assignment will be to make a shoe-box diorama," said Mrs. Troller.

Kids groaned and moaned.

"Aw, man!"

"Nooooo!"

"I hate dioramas."

"I love dioramas!" said Zeke. He does. He even makes them when he doesn't have to. Once he made a diorama of the first time we met, in kindergarten, when I spilled blue paint all over him.

Mrs. Troller ignored the groans and moans.

"You may depict an event or famous person in history, from the years 1500 to 1865."

I had a great idea for my diorama. It was going to be easy to make, I'd get an A, and Annie would be impressed. I would do Emily Dickinson, the poet whose book Annie had been reading on the bus.

I looked Emily Dickinson up on the Internet, because we had to write a page about our diorama. She was a recluse and wrote about 1,800 poems, but only got famous after she died. Sort of like Vincent van Gogh, the artist.

If we had time machines, I'd go tell her.

"Hi, Ms. Dickinson, my name's Tom Marks. I just came from the future in a time machine."

"My goodness! Do all people look like you in the future?"

"No. I'm a Vam-Wolf-Zom. I'm part vampire, werewolf, and zombie. Sorry, sometimes I forget that I'm sort of strange-looking."

"Fret not. The

townspeople here think I am strange because I haven't left my house for many years, see very few people, and like to wear white all the year round. However, I no longer let their opinions cause me pain. I am what I am. I shall not change to please my neighbors."

"Well, I just wanted to tell you that you're world famous in the future. People think you're one of the greatest poets of all time."

"That gladdens my heart. Thank you for telling me. . . . May I compose a poem about you?

"Sure . . ."

"A Vam-Wolf-Zom appeared to Me—
Different, strange, An unusual Fellow—
Just like me? Or so the prying Neighbors say—
Then there are two of us? Hooray!
Others would chase him away like a Mouse—
I should like to invite him for Tea at my house."

It'd be pretty awesome to have a famous poet write a poem about you. So far, the only person who'd written about me was Annie with her song about me spying on her.

I could make the diorama in five minutes because Emma had an old dollhouse with a bunch of furniture I could use. All I'd have to do was put it in a shoebox and add Emily Dickinson. I asked Emma at dinner, in front of Mom and Dad, so they'd make her say yes. That's a good trick.

"Emma, can I borrow some of your old dollhouse furniture for a school project?"

"No," she said automatically, not looking up from her millionth text to Carrot Boy.

She always says "No" when I ask her for anything.

"Why not? All I need is a bed, a chair, a desk, and a dresser."

She looked at me like I'd just asked her to give me her kidney.

"That dollhouse and furniture are a precious part of my childhood. You'll lose them or damage them, and it would break my heart."

Mom rolled her eyes. "Emma, you've tried to sell that dollhouse three times."

Emma said, "That's because one Christmas I had no money and I wanted to buy fabulous gifts for everyone."

Emma Lie #7,654.

"Let your brother use them," said Mom.

"Okay!" said Emma. "I'll rent them to you for five dollars."

"Emma!" said Dad.

I got them for free.

Emma's dollhouse was in the attic. Zeke and I

used to play with it when we were little. We'd have the doll family get murdered and then a detective would come in and solve the case. Our detective was way smarter than Danny the Detective. Or we'd have our plastic dinosaurs attack the people inside. We also had zombie figures pretend to eat them, which is weird to think about now.

I would've used Emma's dollhouse mother for Emily Dickinson, but Muffin, our dog, had actually eaten her. Muffin eats weird stuff.

THINGS MUFFIN HAS EATEN
Legos
Golf ball
Christmas tree ornaments (five)
Emma's retainer

Don't ask how we found out.

Luckily, Emma still had some extra doll clothes, including a white dress that I could put on an old action figure.

I had one called Vacuum Girl, which Emma gave to me for my eighth birthday. She bought it at the Can You Believe It's a Buck? store, where she basically does all her shopping for me.

Vacuum Girl is the worst superhero ever invented. She was a character in this really bad movie that came out like thirty years ago called *Vacuum Girl: A Maid Arises.* I saw it on TV at Zeke's house. He loved it. But he loves every movie he sees.

It was about this teenage girl who worked as a maid at a hotel. One day all these super villains checked in for a super-villain convention. (Which makes no sense.) The girl didn't have any super-powers, but she found a vacuum that could suck people inside it. It had to be plugged into the wall, so she couldn't go very far.

How dumb is that? I could make up a better superhero in like five minutes. I might do that someday.

Zeke fell in love with the actress who played Vacuum Girl. Her name was Keelee Rapose. He even wrote her a fan letter. I couldn't believe it, but she wrote him back and sent a picture signed, "To Zeke, Keep it clean! Love, Keelee." She drew a little heart under her name. Zeke was convinced she was in love with him and they'd get married someday.

"Zeke, you're never even going to meet her!"

"I might. . . . Someday. . . . Maybe."

"You're eight. She's old. I bet she's, like, twenty-five."

"I don't care. Love knows no age."

The Vacuum Girl action figure was almost as bad as the movie. She was dressed in her maid outfit and had a vacuum, but the face didn't look *anything* like the person who played her in the movie. Her eyes were the wrong color, her hair was short and black instead of long and blond, her nose looked like she'd broken it, and she had a scar on her face.

Zeke didn't buy a Vacuum Girl action figure because it didn't look like Keelee.

"Out of respect for Keelee," he said. "I refuse to have it in my house."

The figure was on cardboard backing with a clear plastic cover that read "Talking Vacuum Girl with Her Super Vacuum! She puts villains in the bag! Head swivel action!" I could tell that Emma had tried to peel off the $1.00 sticker, but she had given up.

When you pressed a tiny button on her back, she said some lines from the movie, like, "I'll clean up this mess!" and "You're going in the bag!" and "Does someone need their room cleaned?"

The battery for her voice had already gone dead by the time Emma gave it to me, so she didn't talk anymore. She just made noises that sounded like a cow dying. It was kind of disturbing.

"Why did you get me this, Emma?" I asked when I opened it. "I hated that movie."

"You love superheroes," she said.

"The good ones! Not the lame ones!"

"Sorry, Mr. Picky Particular. Maybe it'll be a collector's item someday."

"I promise you this will *never* be a collector's item."

I didn't even play with it, mainly because I didn't want Emma to think I liked it. I tossed it in the bottom drawer of my desk where I put stuff I don't care about.

०००

When I told Zeke I was going to use Vacuum Girl for my diorama he said, "I wouldn't do that, T-Man. That's an unopened, mint-condition, still-on-the-card action figure. It could be worth, like, a million dollars, even though it doesn't look like Keelee."

Zeke thinks every unopened action figure is worth a million dollars. Vacuum Girl was probably worth exactly what Emma paid for her: one dollar.

The night before the diorama was due, I pulled

the plastic cover off and popped Vacuum Girl out. I took off her maid clothes to put on the white dress.

I got a big surprise.

Vacuum Girl was not who I thought she was.

13.

The Secret of Vacuum Girl

She had a hairy chest and a tattoo on her back that read BIG JACK. The company hadn't even bothered to make a new figure! They'd just used an old character and painted it to look like Vacuum Girl. Big Jack Jackson was a character from a cartoon show my dad used to watch when he was a little kid. It was called *Super Fighting Force Team*.

My dad showed me an episode one time. It was horrible. I didn't say anything because I didn't want him to feel bad. After five minutes, he said, "This isn't as good as I remembered it. In fact, it's really bad, isn't it?"

I nodded.

I wonder if stuff I think is awesome right now will seem dumb or bad when I'm older? I can't worry about that, though. I have too many other things to worry about.

To make the Big Jack figure look like Vacuum Girl, they'd painted on lipstick, eyelashes, and rosy cheeks. No wonder it didn't look like anything like Keelee.

I thought about the person whose job it was to sit there all day and paint the faces. I bet even they knew it looked bad. I wondered if they'd said anything to their boss.

"Hey, Boss? Why are we painting lipstick, eyelashes and rosy cheeks on Big Jack? Is there an episode of Super Fighting Force Team *I didn't see?"*

"He's not Big Jack anymore. It's a new character from a movie called Vacuum Girl. *Start painting."*

"I saw that movie. This doesn't look anything like the person who played that character."

"Don't worry about it. Kids won't tell the difference."

"Yes, they will! Kids are smart. They'll know it looks bad. I won't do it!"

"Get back to work! You have five hundred more Big Jacks to make into Vacuum Girl today!"

"No! I quit! I refuse to make an inferior product! I'm going to become a real artist and do paintings and be rich and famous!"

I wish that had happened, but *somebody* ended up painting all those Big Jacks.

I put the white dress on Vacuum Girl, the action figure formerly known as Big Jack, to turn her into Emily Dickinson. I sat her in a little chair at a desk with a lamp on it, next to a bed.

Emma came by my room to see the diorama.

"Here. I found this." She handed me a miniature typewriter. "It'll look like she's writing a poem."

Emma does random nice things for me sometimes. I'm always surprised.

"Thanks, Emma."

I put the typewriter on the desk. It looked great. I was totally going to get an A.

Little did I know this would turn out to be one of the biggest regrets of my life.

14.

Farewell, My Lovely Emily

The next day at school, everybody put their dioramas on a shelf on one side of Mrs. Troller's room. Zeke's diorama was of Ben Franklin sword fighting with a pirate. He came up with that because I had used the story of Martha Livingston being attacked by a vampire for my history report earlier that year, but I changed it to a pirate. Ben Franklin was stabbing the pirate in the belly and there was blood on the sword and the pirate. I got a little thirsty.

Tanner Gantt's was definitely the *worst*. All he

did was put some dirt in a shoebox, stick in a rock, and put one of those toy pirate ships they use on birthday cakes next to it. It was supposed to be the pilgrims who sailed from England and landed at Plymouth Rock. He hadn't even bothered to take the skull and crossbones pirate flag off the ship.

Tanner was looking at my diorama. He was probably jealous because mine was a million times better than his.

"Is she from your doll collection, Freak Boy?"

I growled at him. I'm not supposed to growl at school, but sometimes I can't help it.

"Mrs. Troller, Tom Marks growled at me!" said Tanner Gantt in a whiny voice.

"No growling please, Tom."

"Sorry, Mrs. Troller."

I turned back to Tanner Gantt. "It's not a doll, it's an action figure." I wanted to add, "And a pirate ship didn't land at Plymouth Rock," but I decided not to. I was hoping Mrs. Troller would notice and give him a bad grade.

"I *love* your diorama, Tom," said Annie.

YES!

"Thanks, Annie."

"Isn't Emily Dickinson's poetry amazing?"

I hadn't actually read any of her poems. "Yeah, it is."

"Where'd you get your Emily Dickinson doll?" she asked.

Zeke leaned in. "It's a Vacuum Girl figure, dressed up like Emily Dickinson."

Tanner Gantt got a weird expression on his face. I thought he was going to say something like, "Only you would have a sucky action figure like Vacuum Girl." But he didn't.

Mrs. Troller looked at all the dioramas.

"Nice job, Mr. Marks." I was so going to get an A. "However, Emily Dickinson didn't use a typewriter. She wrote with a pen."

Tanner Gantt smirked.

"Mr. Gantt," said Mrs. Troller, "I believe it was pilgrims, not pirates, who landed at Plymouth Rock."

Tanner Gantt shrugged. You could tell he didn't care what grade he got. Sometimes I wish I was like that.

Zeke got a B. I got an A minus because my Emily had a typewriter. Tanner Gantt got a C.

For once, life was fair.

It lasted for five minutes.

15.

Mint on Card

After class, I went to dump my history book in my locker. Abel was there, writing his daily quote on our dry-erase board.

"Never spend your money before you have it." —Thomas Jefferson

I told him about my diorama. He raised an eyebrow. "Did you say you used a . . . *Vacuum Girl* action figure?"

"Yeah. Why?"

"I take it you are unaware of her infamous history?"

"You mean how they used an old Big Jack Jackson figure and painted it to look like her?"

Abel smiled. "Ah, that is the mere tip of the iceberg. Walk with me to fourth period and I shall tell you a tale of intrigue, deception, PG-13 violence, shoddy workmanship, and greed."

We walked down the hall and I listened while Abel talked.

"After the Vacuum Girl figure was released, children began cutting themselves on the vacuum cleaner handle and getting the vacuum hose stuck up their nostrils. In addition, the figure had tiny magnets in its hands, which could be dislodged and swallowed. They also used lead paint. Vacuum Girl was declared the most dangerous action figure ever released. They were immediately recalled, removed from stores, and destroyed. Subsequently, very few exist. She is one of the most sought after and valuable action figures in the collecting world."

Abel was like Google. You could ask him about anything.

"How do you know that?" I asked.

"I dabbled in the action figure

market for a brief time. Buying low, selling high. I've attended a few Comic-Cons here and there. There's going to be one at the convention center in January. I may attend for nostalgia's sake, and to assess the current pop culture market."

"So, how much is a Vacuum Girl worth?"

"Well, if you could find one, which is nigh on impossible, and it was un-opened, still on the card, and in mint condition, they have been known to fetch upward of fifteen hundred dollars."

"WHAT?!"

I almost fainted for the third time in my life. Zeke had been *right*. I shouldn't have used Vacuum Girl. I have to start listening to him.

I couldn't believe that cheap, ugly, badly made figure was worth that much. Emma had been right too, when she said it might be a collector's item someday. I hate it when Emma is right.

"What about if it's been opened?" I asked Abel.

"Due to the rarity, she would still be worth a pretty penny. I would venture to say at least a thousand dollars."

I raced back to Mrs. Troller's room using my vam-wolf speed. As I ran down the hall, dodging and zigzagging around the slowest people in the world, I started to make a list of the stuff I could get with the money.

1. Five new video games
2. New skateboard
3. Giant TV for my room
4. A good microphone for our band

I shoved some kids out of the way in front of Mrs. Troller's classroom. She looked up from her desk.

"What's the matter, Tom?"

"Nothing, I hope!"

I ran over to my diorama on the shelf.

The rocking chair was empty.

Emily Dickinson, also known as Vacuum Girl, also known as Big Jack Jackson, was gone.

16.

Whodunit?

Maybe some kid bumped into the diorama and she fell out of her rocking chair onto the floor. Or maybe somebody put her in another diorama for a joke.

I looked on the floor, behind the shelf, under the shelf, behind my diorama, and in every other diorama. Emily was nowhere to be seen. Did someone know how much she was worth? I got a bad feeling in my stomach.

"Mrs. Troller, somebody stole Emily Dickinson."

"Why would someone do that?" she asked. "Is it valuable?"

I had to play my cards right.

"Uh . . . My sister bought it at the Can You Believe It's Only a Buck? store."

Mrs. Troller turned toward the kids who were sitting down for fourth period.

"Has anyone seen the Emily Dickinson figure from Tom Marks's diorama?"

They all shook their heads. But one of them was lying. I looked at each face, searching for a clue as to whom the guilty party was.

Bridgid O'Shaughnessy's left eye was twitching. It was her! But then she reached up with her fingers and took a contact lens out of her eye, blinked a few times, and put it back in. I crossed her off the suspect list.

Elliot Friedman was nervously crossing and uncrossing his legs. Maybe he took Emily? Or maybe he just had to go to the bathroom? He spends a lot of time in the restrooms.

Jason Gruber's eyes shifted back and forth like he was hiding something. But maybe he was just looking over at Emily Arbon. He has a gigantic crush on her.

I saw David Landis slowly put his hand into his shirt pocket. Was Emily in there? He pulled out his retainer and put it in his mouth.

I looked at Olivia Dunaway. Most people thought she was the prettiest girl in the sixth grade. Maybe in the whole school. She was looking at me like she wanted to invite me to her next birthday party. I smiled at her. She smiled back, and when she tilted her head to the side, her long, dark hair fell across her face. I crossed her off the suspect list.

Mrs. Troller said, "Tom, you need to get to fourth period. I'll keep an eye out for Emily Dickinson."

Would she? Could I trust Mrs. Troller? Could I trust anybody?

I wanted to interrogate the whole class, like tough private detectives do in those old movies my Dad loves. I know exactly what I'd say:

"Okay, listen up. If anybody here thinks Emily Dickinson is going home with them, that is not going to happen. Hand her over right now or it's going to get ugly. And when I say ugly, I mean Grumpy Janitor is going to have to come in here afterward, with his mop and bucket, and clean up a big mess. So, I'm not leaving this room until the person who stole Emily confesses and I've got her back. Safe and sound and in mint condition. Empty your pockets, purses, and backpacks. And I don't need a search warrant. I've got my search warrant right here. They're called razor-sharp fangs."

I wish I could've said that to them. But I didn't.

"Tom?" said Mrs. Troller. "Why are you still here? You need to get to your next class or you'll be tardy."

I looked up at the clock. She wasn't lying—I needed to go. And I needed to think. As I walked out, I took one last look at Emily's empty chair in the diorama. Would she ever sit in it again?

17.

Shadow of a Doubt

I walked down the empty hallway. I heard a saxophone playing a sad, bluesy melody that matched my mood. I felt like I was in a movie. Then, I realized I was walking by the band room. Through the door, I saw Dani Michaeli practicing his saxophone. He was good. I bet he'd try out for the talent show in January. Our band was going to try out too. But I couldn't think about that now. I had to find Emily before somebody sold her and I never saw her again.

I needed a drink. My mouth felt as dry as the

kindergartner sand box. I stopped at a drinking fountain. As I took a long drink of cool, clear water, I went over the facts in my head. All the kids in Mrs. Troller's third period had heard Zeke say that Emily Dickinson was Vacuum Girl. Did any of them know she was valuable? Did any kid in Troller's fourth-period class know who Emily really was? That was two whole classes of possible suspects. I couldn't rule out anybody. Even Mrs. Troller. Did she collect action figures? Is that why she assigned the dioramas, hoping that someday, someone would bring in a Vacuum Girl?

I headed to class, still running the case over in my mind. The last time I'd seen Emily, she was sitting at her desk as I went out the door, when third period ended. I was the last person to leave, so nobody in that class had stolen her. It had to be somebody in fourth period—Wait. I *wasn't* the last person to leave. There was somebody by the windows putting on their backpack.

Tanner Gantt.

It was him. He'd stolen Zeke's skateboard and probably a million other things. He became my number one suspect.

I pushed open the door and walked into Math class just after the tardy bell rang. I explained to Ms. Heckroth what had happened. I thought she'd give me a break, but she didn't care that a major crime had been committed. She handed me a pink tardy slip.

Next period, in Art class, I slumped down into my seat beside Capri. She stopped drawing the falcon she was sketching, put down her pencil, and looked over at me with her dark, brown eyes.

"Sorry to hear about Emily Dickinson," she said.

"How'd you hear about it?"

"Bad news spreads fast at Hamilton."

"Yeah. Just like lice."

Zeke had lice when we were in first grade. Capri and I both got it from him, so she knew what I was talking about and nodded. Did werewolves get lice? I hoped not.

"Is there anything I can do to help?" she asked.

"I don't think so."

She put her hand on my arm. That was weird. But sort of nice at the same time.

"Well, if you think of anything," she said. "Let me know."

The lunch bell rang and I was zombie-hungry. I got over to the cafeteria as fast as I could. I was first in line. Fair and square. I didn't cut. I wasn't going to risk The Table of Shame again. I could see Liversidge across the room, watching me like a hawk.

"What'll you have, Tom?" asked Lunch Lady. "The usual?"

"Yeah. Make it a double."

She handed over a double cheeseburger, rare, and French fries, extra crispy.

"What're you drinking today?" she asked.

"Milk. You got a cold one from the back of the fridge?"

"Yep. And it's got your name on it."

She put an ice-cold carton of milk down on the silver counter.

"Make it two," I said.

A second carton joined the first. They looked like twins.

"Rough day, Tom?"

"You could say so. Somebody stole something from me."

"Sorry to hear that."

"The person who stole it is going to be sorry too, when I find them."

I have to admit, it was sort of cool, acting like an old-school detective.

Lunch Lady gave me a look that said, *I'll never steal anything from you*.

I cracked open the first milk carton, slid the straw in, and took a long sip. It tasted bitter. Sour. Rotten. Exactly the way I felt. I looked at the expiration date. It had expired six months ago. Just my luck.

A bad day was about to get worse.

18.

Reasonable Suspicion

As we sat at our usual table in the cafeteria, I told Abel, Zeke, Annie, and Capri that I thought Tanner Gantt had stolen Emily. I let Abel tell them how much she was worth. I could trust them. They were my friends.

Dog Hots let out a low, long whistle.

"That's a lot of money for a piece of plastic," said Annie.

"I have a Baby Bobby Bear collection that's worth a fortune," said Capri.

Abel frowned. "Sorry to be the bearer of bad

news, no pun intended, but they made millions of Baby Bobby Bears. They are currently worth about a dollar apiece. But I'm sure you had many hours of delight playing with them."

Capri said a word I'd never heard her say before.

Abel went on. "If it's any consolation, the person who stole Emily or Vacuum Girl or Big Jack doesn't have her maid uniform, hat, apron, or most importantly, her dangerous vacuum cleaner. So, they would get some money selling it, but not a lot."

"True," I said. "But I won't get a dime. And if it's Tanner Gantt, that just makes it worse."

Abel nodded. "He is a prime suspect. However, the possibility does exist that he doesn't know how valuable Vacuum Girl is. He may have just absconded with Emily as a typical act of aggression against you."

"Or maybe he has an Emily Dickinson collection?" suggested Zeke.

We all rolled our eyes.

"Why don't you just ask Tanner Gantt if he stole it?" asked Capri.

I shook my head. "I want to be careful, in case he doesn't know how much she's worth. I don't want to make him suspicious."

Abel rested his chin on his hands. "'Tis a conundrum."

I didn't know what "conundrum" meant, so I asked Abel. I used to not do that when people said words I didn't know, so people wouldn't think I was dumb. But it was dumber not to ask.

Abel explained. "A 'conundrum' is a puzzle, a mystery, or a problem."

"That's a good name for a band!" said Zeke. "We should call ourselves Conundrum."

Everyone thought about it for a minute, and we agreed it was a good name. That was the first time we had agreed on anything.

"Look who's here," said Dog Hots. Tanner Gantt had just walked into the cafeteria.

Annie put down her grilled cheese sandwich and stood up. "I'll find out if he took it."

I had a mouthful of cheeseburger, so I couldn't say anything. By the time I swallowed and said, "Wait! Annie! No!" she was already in Tanner Gantt's face.

"What's your problem, Barstow?" he sneered.

"Did you steal Tom's Emily Dickinson?"

"Why would I want a stupid doll?"

"Maybe you have an Emily Dickinson collection," said Zeke, as the rest of us rolled our eyes again and walked up behind Annie.

She wasn't giving up. "If you don't have her, prove it. Let me look in your backpack."

"No way," he said.

"Okay. Then, maybe I'll go ask Principal Gonzales to take a look."

"He can't legally do that."

"Why not?" demanded Annie.

"The Bill of Rights. It protects people from unlawful searches."

How did Tanner Gantt know that? He never paid attention in class.

"Oh, really?" said Annie, with a smile. "In 1985 the Supreme Court said school officials do not need probable cause or a warrant to search students if there is reasonable suspicion."

I bet Annie ends up on the Supreme Court someday.

Tanner Gantt crossed his big arms and said, "The court also said they can only search a backpack if there is an 'urgent risk to the safety of other students.' How is a missing Emily Dickinson action figure a risk?" He waved and walked away, smirking. "Bye-bye."

Annie sat down and shook her head. "Sometimes, I hate the Supreme Court."

"I have a suggestion, Mr. Marks," said Abel.

"Perhaps you could make a flyer and offer a reward for the safe return of Ms. Dickinson?"

"That's a great idea." I put down my half-eaten cheeseburger. "Capri, can you draw a picture of my action figure?"

She pulled out a pen and twirled it in her fingers. "I can draw *anything*."

19.

Missing Persons

Capri did a great drawing. There were about fifteen minutes left of lunch period, so Zeke and I ran to the library to print up some flyers. Ms. Paroo, the librarian, looked suspicious when we asked her.

"What is this for *exactly*?"

"It's for Mrs. Troller's History class," I said. That was half true. She bought it.

Have You Seen Me?

Missing: Emily Dickinson

5 ½" tall. Short brown hair. Crossed brown eyes. Heavy eyebrows.

Scar on cheek. Large nose.

Last seen on December 1st, 11:23 AM, in Room 222, third period, in a shoebox, wearing a white dress and sitting at a desk with a typewriter.

Generous reward for her safe and undamaged return or for any information leading to the arrest, prosecution, and super-long jail sentence for whoever stole her.

Contact: Tom Marks

We'd only put up about fifteen flyers when Principal Gonzales saw us and said we had to take them all down.

"Gentlemen, you need permission to put up flyers at school."

I gave him a big, fake Maren Nesmith smile. "Can we please have your permission?"

"Sorry. They have to be related to school activities." He looked at the flyer. "I had an action figure collection when I was about your age. Pretty big one. My mother gave them all away when I went to college. Worth a lot of money now. But—"

I didn't have time to hear Principal Gonzales's life story.

"We'd better get to class," I said.

He reached out his hand. "I'll take those."

We gave him the flyers and he walked off.

Zeke had his I've Got a Crazy Idea, but I'm Going to Tell You Anyway expression.

"T-Man. . . . Maybe Principal Gonzales stole Vacuum Girl. Maybe he told us to take down the flyers so no one would see them. Maybe he and Mrs. Troller operate a secret, underground action-figure crime organization. She tells him if a kid brings a valuable figure to school, they steal them, and then they sell them!"

"I don't think so, Zeke."

We decided to return to the scene of the crime to see if anyone had turned Emily in. We had five minutes before the sixth-period tardy bell rang. As we got closer, I smelled a hot Italian sausage sandwich with cheese, grilled peppers, and onions. I hadn't finished my double cheeseburger, so I was hungry. And when you're one-third zombie, you have to be careful not to get hungry.

Mrs. Troller was at her desk. In front of her was half of the greatest-smelling sandwich in the world.

"Sorry, Tom. No one's turned her in."

I stared at her sandwich. It smelled so good I almost started drooling. Luckily, Mrs. Troller noticed.

"Would you like the other half of this, Tom? I can't finish the whole thing."

"Really? Thanks, Mrs. Troller."

I took the sandwich and was just about to take a bite when Zeke grabbed my arm.

"T-Man! I know how you can find Emily Dickinson!"

"How?"

"Use your werewolf sense of smell."

"But I don't know what she smells like."

"Smell her chair!"

I sniffed the chair in the diorama. It smelled like old wood, but there was another smell too. Plastic. I went back out in the hall and sniffed the air. I could smell the same scent, faintly, in the distance. We took off toward it and I ate the sandwich on the way.

It was hard to separate Vacuum Girl's smell from everything else I could smell: the sausage sandwich, different girls' perfumes, hair gels, fresh paint on a door that Grumpy Janitor was painting, kids who should be using deodorant but weren't.

I followed the scent to where it got more intense. We were getting close. I would've bet a million dollars I would end up at Tanner Gantt's locker. We came around a corner, and there was Dog Hots, holding something in his hand.

Dog Hots had stolen Emily.

I walked up to him. "I thought you were my friend!"

"What're you talking about?" he said.

"We're in a band together! My dad let you use his drum set!"

"What's wrong with you, Marks?"

"Hand her over!"

"Hand *who* over?"

"Emily Dickinson!"

"I don't have her!"

"Oh, yeah? What's in your hand?"

He opened his hand. He was holding a Dr. Bad Brains action figure.

I bent down and sniffed it. Who knew all action figures smelled alike?

"Oh. . . . Sorry, Dog Hots," I said. "It was a simple case of mistaken identity."

I felt like my name was Danny the Detective. He made stupid mistakes like that.

When we got to Phys Ed, I had some important business to attend to.

20.

The Informer

I was in the restroom, doing what you do in there, when I heard a voice I didn't recognize come from the next stall.

"Marks?"

"Yeah?"

"I hear you're looking for somebody."

"I might be."

Whoever it was must've seen one of our flyers before Principal Gonzales made us take them down.

"I hear it's a certain female who wore white

dresses, didn't leave her house, and wrote eighteen hundred poems."

This kid knew a lot about Emily Dickinson.

"Go on," I said.

"I just might happen to know her present location."

"Where is she?"

"What's it worth to you?"

"Five dollars?"

"Forget it. You must not want her back very badly."

"Okay, okay. Ten dollars. What do you know?"

"Slow down. Let's see the green paper with Mr. Hamilton's picture on it first."

I reached into my front jean pocket, which, considering my current position, wasn't easy. I started to hand the money under the stall, but stopped.

"Wait. . . . How do I know your information is real?"

"I heard a kid talking to another kid behind the cafeteria."

Behind the cafeteria was where some kids ate lunch and supposedly did things you're not supposed to do at school. Emma had warned me, "Never eat lunch behind the cafeteria."

"And you're *sure* they were talking about Emily Dickinson?" I asked.

"He wasn't talking about Wonder Woman."

"Did he actually say 'Emily Dickinson'?"

"No. He's too smart for that. He said he had something very valuable, stolen from a classroom, and he was willing to sell it."

"Are you talking about Hammet Chandler?" said a new voice from the stall on the other side of me.

"Mind your own business!" said the first voice.

"Hammet wasn't talking about Emily Dickinson, he was selling answers to Ms. Heckroth's math test on Friday."

"How do you know?" I asked.

"Because I bought them from him."

"Oh. . . . Thanks," I said, to whoever had just saved me ten bucks.

"No problem. . . . Hey, you want to buy some test answers?"

"No thanks," I said.

"I do!" said the first kid.

I went out of the stall. The other kids stayed and finished their business.

21.

Tailing Tanner Gantt

After choir, I took the bus home, but Suspect #1, Tanner Gantt, didn't. The bus passed him as he walked down the sidewalk. I lowered my window and took a sniff. I smelled Cheetos, beef jerky, a book, and some clothes that needed washing. But I still had a hunch that he had Emily. I had to find out for sure.

I got off the bus, ran home, dumped my backpack, and raced over to Tanner Gantt's house. I caught up with him just as he was walking into his backyard. I watched from behind the wooden fence as he walked past his empty swimming pool. His big, mean, ugly dog came roaring out the doggie door, barking like he wanted to kill somebody.

"Shut up, Max! It's just me!"

Max saw who it was and shut up.

Tanner Gantt petted Max and then he bent over and kissed the top of his big, ugly head. I didn't think he'd do something like that. I also didn't think he'd know about the Bill of Rights either. People surprise you sometimes.

Tanner and Max went in the house through the back door.

I quietly opened the gate in the fence and crossed the yard, avoiding Max's piles of poop. I counted six. I crept up to a window and peeked into the kitchen. It was a mess, with dirty dishes piled up in the sink and on the table. Tanner Gantt pulled off his backpack and dropped it on the floor. If Emily was in there, I hoped she wasn't getting banged up.

"Tanner?" said a sleepy woman's voice from another room.

"Mom?" he called back, sounding surprised. "Why aren't you at work?"

"I'm . . . sick."

"Again?"

"Yes! Bring me a Diet Coke!"

He opened the fridge, grabbed a can of Diet Coke, and walked out of the room.

Here was my chance. I opened the back door, went over to the backpack, and unzipped it.

"In a glass with ice!" yelled his mom.

I heard Tanner Gantt mumble a bad word. He turned around and headed back to the kitchen. I had to act fast.

"Turn to bat, bat I shall be!" I whispered.

Bam.

I was a bat. I flew inside the backpack to hide, just as he walked in. If Emily was in there, I'd wait until he took the drink to his mom, grab her, and get out. As I heard him open the freezer to get some ice cubes, I took a look around his backpack.

There wasn't much. An old pair of headphones. Math and history books. Two crumpled Cheetos bags. Half of a jalapeño beef jerky stick that looked like it had been in there since fourth grade. And at the bottom, a stinky, sweaty, rolled-up T-shirt. It smelled so bad I almost puked. Having a super sense of smell is not always a good thing.

Tanner Gantt hadn't stolen Emily. Now I had to wait until he left the room, so I could get out of there.

But then, I smelled something else. The faint smell of plastic.

I quietly and carefully unrolled the T-shirt.

Hello, Emily.

22.

Trapped

There she was, looking up at me. Unharmed and in mint condition. I hadn't smelled her because his stinky T-shirt had overpowered it. Had Tanner Gantt done that on purpose? Was he smarter than I thought? I didn't want to consider that possibility. I had Emily—I mean, Vacuum Girl—and as soon as he left the room I'd take her home.

Footsteps.

I mean, paw steps.

Max trotted into the kitchen and started to

sniff the backpack. His big nose was pushing right up against me on the other side of the nylon material. He barked.

"Shut up, Max!" yelled Tanner Gantt.

Max kept barking.

"Max! Shut! Up!"

Max wasn't going to stop. He smelled a bat. If Darcourt had taught me how to talk to dogs, I could've whispered to him:

"Max, listen to your master. Stop barking."

"Who said that?"

"My name's Tom. I'm a Vam-Wolf-Zom. But right now I'm a bat."

"What . . . ? I'm confused."

"Don't worry about it, Max. Just go away."

"I never ate a bat before."

"You don't want to. They taste horrible."

"I'm starving! I haven't had my dinner."

"Well, that's because you have a bad master. He's a jerk, a bully, he lies, he's mean, and he steals things."

"Don't say those things about my master!"

"Well, I'm sorry. But it's the truth. Please, Max. Go. Away."

"You're not the boss of me. I'm going to rip open this backpack with my teeth and eat you."

"No! Don't! I can tell, just from talking to you, that you won't like the taste of bat."

"Well, my mother always told me, 'Don't be a picky eater.'"

Maybe it's better I can't talk to dogs.

Luckily, I heard Tanner Gantt drag Max out of the room to some other part of the house. A door closed, and then Tanner came back alone. I still had to wait for him to leave the room so I could escape.

"Tanner, what is taking you so long?"

His mom came in the kitchen. It sounded like she was standing right next to the backpack.

"How was school?"

"Fine."

"No video games or TV 'til you do your homework."

"I did it on the bus home."

"Show me."

"Why?"

"'Cause I don't believe you. Where is it? In here?"

She picked up the backpack.

No, no, no, no, no! You don't need to look in here! Trust your son! I put Emily on top of the stinky T-shirt and slid underneath it *just* as she looked inside.

"I don't see any homework in here, Tanner."

"I just had to read some chapters in those books."

I felt her pick up Emily.

"What're you doing with a doll?"

"It's for History class. I have to do a diorama about Emily Dickinson."

"She didn't win any beauty contests, did she? I should give this to Allison. She likes dolls."

No! No! No! Don't give it to Allison! It has lead paint! It has magnets! It'll kill poor Allison, whoever she is.

"Who's Allison?" asked Tanner Gantt.

"She's Jerry's little daughter."

"Who's Jerry?"

"I told you about him, Tanner. The nice man who's gonna give me that job at the mall for the holidays."

"I haven't done my diorama yet. So, I gotta use it now."

"Okay! Do your diorama, then I'm giving it to Allison."

I felt Emily land on top of the T-shirt. She'd dropped her back in.

"*What* is that smell, Tanner? That T-shirt is disgusting. This has gotta be washed, right now."

Nooooo! Don't wash the T-shirt! Leave it there!

"Okay, okay. I will. What's for dinner?"

She dropped the backpack on the floor.

"There's pizza in the freezer. I'm going out tonight."

"I thought you were sick?"

"I was—I am. I'm going to sleep more and I'll feel better."

I heard her walk away.

Tanner picked up the backpack, walked a bit,

and then stopped. I heard a handle turn, a door open and close, and then a lock turn. His hand reached inside the backpack and took out Emily. He tossed the backpack onto the floor. I heard him at a computer, typing.

I slid out from under the stinky T-shirt, and carefully crawled up to peek out the top of the backpack. I was looking at Tanner Gantt's room.

23.

The Secret World of Tanner Gantt

He was sitting at a desk with his back to me. I bet he was putting Vacuum Girl up on eBay. She was next to him, still dressed as Emily, propped up against a lamp on the desk. When he turned to look at her, I got a big surprise.

Tanner Gantt wore glasses.

He'd never worn them at school. He always made fun of people with glasses.

Tanner's phone was on speaker and someone's voice mail kicked in.

"This is Hannigan. You better have a good reason for calling me."

Beep.

"It's Tanner. I got that thing I told you about. Call me when you want me to bring it over. And then we'll be even, and I won't owe you any more money."

He hung up.

I knew who he'd called. It was an older kid named Dennis Hannigan. He was basically the scariest, meanest, toughest person at Emma's high school.

I looked around the room. "Tanner Rules!" was spray-painted in black paint on one wall. My parents would *kill me* if I did that. I guess his mom didn't care.

He had some posters on the other walls: a skateboarding guy with long hair, some wrestler named Mister Mess You Up Bad, and a band called King Moe, who looked like the angriest three guys in the world. Like they might kill you if you didn't like their music. There was another poster of a red-haired woman in the smallest bathing suit I have ever seen in my life. My mom wouldn't let me put something like that up in a million years.

There was a silver baseball bat next to some weights, which he probably used to get muscles for beating up people. There was an old, black bass guitar on the bed. He'd probably stolen the bass and was planning to sell it.

Then, I got a surprise bigger than the glasses.

There was a bookshelf jammed with books. Not as many as Annie had in her bedroom, but a lot. *Tanner Gantt read books?* That explained how he knew about the Bill of Rights. I never would have guessed that in a million years.

And under his bed I saw an old stuffed animal. It was an elephant. I couldn't imagine Tanner Gantt playing with it, but I guess he was a baby at some point. I wondered if he was a mean baby.

I waited and watched, peeking out of the backpack. Tanner played a video game called World War Ten. I have to admit, he was pretty good.

Meanwhile, I was getting zombie-hungry. I decided to eat the spicy sweet jalapeño beef jerky. It wasn't bad. But it wasn't enough to fill me up. I had to get home. I saw out Tanner's window that the sun had gone down. I needed a plan.

Get Vacuum Girl and Escape Plan

1. Fly out of the backpack and turn back into me. (But then Tanner Gantt would know I could turn into a bat.)
2. Stay a bat. (He'd still probably know the bat was me.)
3. Take Vacuum Girl and leave fast so his mom didn't see me. (Risky—she kept showing up.)

I heard the door handle jiggle.

"Tanner!" said his mom. "Why's your door locked?"

"So I can have some privacy!"

"What're you doing in there?"

"I'm working on my diorama."

"It's trash night. Take the barrels out."

"I *will*."

"Do it now. You'll forget like you did last week and I had to do it. I broke a nail and I just had them done!"

"You are always tired or sick! I have to do everything!"

"Don't talk to me like that or you will regret it big-time!"

I heard her walk away down the hall.

No wonder Tanner Gantt liked to go and sit on the swings in the park at night. I would too if my mom yelled at me like that. I felt kind of sorry for him, but not too much. He was still a thief and a bully.

I was lucky it was trash night. Here was my chance to escape.

Tanner Gantt stood up, unlocked his door, and walked out. I flew out of the backpack and over to the desk, and grabbed Emily by her head with my feet. Or were they claws? Or talons? I had to look that up. I should know the names of my body parts.

I flew by the door and hovered, looking down the hall. The coast was clear. I flew out of the room, turned into the kitchen, and slammed right into his mom's face.

24.

Did You Say "Bat"?

Tanner Gantt's mom said the same swear word three times and then started screaming.

"Tanner! Help!"

I was hoping she'd run away, but she didn't. She called me a lot of names that I'd only heard in R-rated movies. She started swatting at me with her hands, and knocked Emily out of my grip. The doll fell to the floor.

"Tanner! Get in here!"

I heard him running into the house. I flew

behind a big box of Sugar Bombs cereal on the refrigerator just as Tanner ran into the kitchen.

"What's the matter?!"

"Kill it! Kill it! Kill it!"

"Kill what?"

"The bat!"

"Bat? Did you say 'bat'?"

"Yes! I said bat!" yelled his Mom. "Kill it!"

"There's a bat in here?"

"Yes! How many times do I have to say it? What is wrong with you?!"

"Are you sure it's a bat?"

"Yes! I'm sure! It tried to peck my eyes out and bite me! I could've gotten rabies!"

"Where is it?"

"I think it flew behind the cereal on the fridge."

From where I was hiding, I could see Emily lying on the floor. Luckily, Tanner Gantt hadn't noticed her yet. But he would. I had to get her and get out of there. Fast.

"Stay here, Tanner," said his mom. "I'll get your baseball bat and you can smash it!"

I didn't like the sound of that plan. His mom ran out of the room. I heard the floor creak as Tanner took two steps toward the refrigerator.

"Marks?" he said. "Is that you? Are you a bat?"

I heard his mom run back in. She brought Max too, barking his head off. A giant dog trying to eat me would make it even harder to escape.

"Here's your bat, Tanner! Smash him!"

It was now or never. I flew out from behind the Sugar Bombs box, staying close to the ceiling. His mom was still holding the baseball bat and she took a swing at me. Apparently she had not played much baseball because she swung wide and almost hit her son.

"Mom! You almost killed me!"

Tanner Gantt ducked and grabbed the bat from her. I flew around him and swooped down to the floor. I dodged Max, who tried to eat me, picked up Emily, and flew out through the doggie door flap.

Freedom!

I flew across the backyard, over the fence, and headed home. I stayed low, keeping an eye out for owls. Finally I landed in my backyard, put Emily in the grass, and changed back into me. I gently picked her up and looked down at her resting in my hand.

"You're safe now."

But our troubles weren't over.

25.

The Highest Bidder

When I walked into the kitchen, Mom was in her I Am Very Mad at You position, with both fists on her hips.

"Where have you been, young man?"

I sat down. "It's a long story."

"I'd like to hear it," she said.

"Me too," said Emma, with a big smile. She loves it when I get in trouble.

I said I was doing homework at a kid from school's house, which was partially true. I apologized and told her that next time I'd call.

"What grade did you get on your Emily Dickinson diorama?" asked Emma.

"A minus. I would've gotten an A, but the real Emily didn't use a typewriter."

Emma shrugged. "I'm not a historian."

I went upstairs and put Emily, who was going to turn back into Vacuum Girl soon, in my bottom desk drawer. I'd put her up for sale online tomorrow night at six. Mom always said that was the best time to sell stuff.

The next morning, Tanner Gantt got on the bus, walked down the aisle to where I was sitting, and stopped.

"So . . . you figured out how to turn into a bat."

I didn't say anything. I just looked at him.

"It's about freaking time," he said, then walked to the back of the bus and sat down.

o o o

At home after school, I put Vacuum Girl's maid uniform, hat, and apron back on her. Luckily, I hadn't thrown away the cardboard backing and the plastic bubble cover. I attached her back onto the card, next to the vacuum, and glued the plastic cover on. She still smelled like the beef jerky from Tanner Gantt's backpack.

I took some pictures and put her up for auction online. I got a lot of bids right away. By the end of the week, she sold for $1,154.76 to a woman in Japan named Ginger. She was president of The International Vacuum Girl Fan Club. I couldn't believe they had a club.

In a weird way, I was sorry to see Vacuum Girl go. But all that money made it easy. I was going to buy so many awesome things.

I laid out some bubble wrap, tape, and scissors next to Vacuum Girl on my bed, and I went downstairs to get a mailing box from the garage. When I came back upstairs, Muffin trotted past me in the hallway. Out of the corner of my eye, I saw he had something in his mouth. I stopped and turned around.

"Muffin?"

He stopped.

"*Muffin . . . ?*"

He slowly turned to look at me.

That's when I saw her head sticking out, between his teeth.

Muffin was eating Vacuum Girl.

"No! Muffin! Drop it!"

Why couldn't I speak dog, like Darcourt? I would've said, "Muffin, drop that right now and I'll give you *anything* you want to eat for the rest of your life!" I was beginning to regret not joining the wolf pack.

I slowly moved toward Muffin. He knew what I was doing, and he ran off. I chased him down the stairs and finally caught him in the kitchen, just as he was about to go out the doggie door. I grabbed him, pried open his jaws, and got Emily out.

I closed my eyes and quietly said to myself, "Please don't be chewed up."

Hopefully, she just had dog slobber on her. I could clean her up. I opened my eyes and looked.

I said a bad word.

Her head was barely attached to her neck. There were teeth marks all over her body, and her face was chewed up. Even Zeke wouldn't recognize her.

Goodbye, video games. Goodbye, skateboard. Goodbye, giant TV. Goodbye, Emily, Vacuum Girl, and Big Jack.

It was Muffin's fault for eating her, Tanner's fault for stealing her, Emma's fault for having the dollhouse that gave me the idea, Emily's fault for being a famous poet whom Annie loved, and Mrs. Troller's fault for assigning those stupid dioramas.

Nobody would want a chewed-up, mangled, twisted Vacuum Girl. I e-mailed Ginger and explained what happened. She didn't believe me at first, so I sent her pictures. She wrote me back.

> Dear Mr. Tom Marks,
>   Please forgive my doubting you. I was heartbroken to see our beautiful Vacuum Girl destroyed. Please do not blame your Muffin dog, he did not know what he was doing. I hope to see you at our We Love Vacuum Girl So Much Fan Club Convention next year in Tokyo or at the next Comic-Con!
>   "Keep It Clean!"
>   Ginger Kurosawa
>   President and
> Founder of We
> Love Vacuum Girl   So
> Much Fan Club

"Aw, man," said Zeke, when I showed him chewed-up Vacuum Girl over the phone.

"I should've listened to you, Zeke. I never should've unwrapped her and used her for that stupid diorama."

He shrugged. Zeke never says stuff like "I told you so!" or "Yeah! You should have listened to me, you stupid idiot!" I appreciate that.

"Are you going to bury her?" he asked.

"No."

Zeke used to bury his action figures once they got broken. He had a whole cemetery in his back-yard.

"What're you going to do with her, T-Man?"

"Throw her away. She's just junk now."

"Um. . . . Can I have her?"

"Seriously?"

"She looks like a cool mutant or an alien. Or like she got exposed to atomic radiation."

"Or a dog tried to eat her," I said.

"Yeah! A giant prehistoric dinosaur dog!"

"You really want her, Zeke?"

"I do!"

"She's yours."

Zeke smiled like I'd given him an awesome gift. "Excellent!"

o o o

That night, I was in my room getting ready for bed. I was singing one of our band songs, practicing the harmony. All of a sudden, I had a creepy feeling that someone was watching me. I looked up and saw two small, green eyes outside my window. A very familiar-looking bat was sitting on my windowsill.

Martha Livingston was back.

26.

A Surprise Visitor

How long had she been there? I felt like Annie must've felt when I looked in her bedroom. I went over and lifted up the window.

"Good evening, Thomas Marks."

"Were you spying on me?"

"Yes."

She flew in. By the time I'd closed the window and turned around, she'd transformed into herself. I'd forgotten how long and red her hair was. She was wearing a blue dress this time. She held her

hand out to me and I shook it. It was cold, but
really soft.

"May I have my hand back?" she said.

I let go. "Oh. Sorry. How long were you watching me?"

"Long enough. I must say, you have a voice to
be proud of."

"Thanks." I didn't remember her eyes being so
green.

She looked around the room. "Is your bedchamber always this untidy?"

"I . . . I was just about to clean it up."

She smirked. "Of course you were. So, I am here to check in on you. How have you fared since we last set eyes upon each other on All Hallows' Eve?"

"Okay."

"And how are your girlfriends, Annie and Capri? Has either won your heart?"

"They are *not* my girlfriends!"

She sat down in my desk chair and slowly swiveled it back and forth. "How go your lessons?"

I shrugged. "School's okay, I guess."

"I meant your *vampiric* lessons."

"Oh . . ."

"Surely you have learned to transform to smoke, at least?"

"Not yet."

"Good Lord! Why did I entrust you with the book in the first place?"

"Sorry, but I've had a ton of stuff to do for school."

"As Dr. Franklin said, 'Never ruin an apology with an excuse.'"

She was always quoting Benjamin Franklin.

"Can you help me?" I asked.

"Show me what you are doing."

I took a deep breath and tried to turn to smoke *ten times* and couldn't do it.

"'Tis a conundrum," she said. "Possibly you are trying too hard?"

"How long did it take you to learn?"

"A few days."

"Do you think it's because I'm only one-third vampire?"

"Perhaps. . . . However, you shouldn't let that stop you."

I decided to change the subject. "How was that vampire-gathering thing that you went to in New Orleans?"

"There was quite a bit of interest in the world's only Vam-Wolf-Zom. Many wish to come and meet you."

I got a horrible feeling in my stomach. "You didn't bring any other vampires with you?" I ran to the window to look out.

There wasn't anybody on the front lawn. Or in the trees. Or hovering in the sky.

Martha sighed. "I brought no vampires. . . . How fares your friend, Zeke? Does he continue to refrain from doing jumping jacks when excited?"

"Yeah. . . . Hey, can you reverse hypnotize somebody?"

She raised an eyebrow. "I know not what you mean."

"I kind of miss him doing them. If I wanted him to do jumping jacks again, could I get him to?"

"You have learned a valuable lesson. Changing another's nature has unseen consequences. Yes, you may hypnotize Zeke and tell him to commence jumping jacks. Has anything else of importance transpired since we last spoke?"

I'd forgotten the most important thing.

"Oh! Yeah. I met Darcourt, the werewolf."

She jumped out of the chair.

"What? Where? When?"

"In the woods at my gram's, on Thanksgiving."

"Did you flee as I instructed?"

"Uh. . . No."

"You fought him?"

"No!"

"Tell me what occurred. Spare no detail."

"We just hung out for a while. I asked him about being a werewolf. He wasn't at all like you described him."

"Darcourt is a master deceiver. He puts on many faces and personalities. Do not be fooled. He is not what he seems."

"He didn't seem dangerous to me. He was really nice and friendly."

"The most dangerous usually are. What else happened?"

"He wanted to see the book you lent me."

Her eyes got big. You told him you had a copy of *A Vampiric Education*?!"

"Uh. . . . Yeah."

"You dunderhead!"

I knew she'd call me that eventually.

"*Please* tell me you did not show it to him!"

"I didn't. But he really wanted to see it."

"Of course he did! Any werewolf would, in order to learn our ways. Is the book safe? Well hidden?"

"Yeah."

I decided not to tell her I'd told Darcourt where I hid it. I still needed to hide it in a new place.

Instead I said, "Martha, I read what Lovick Zabrecky wrote in the book, where he said he'd do horrible things if you gave it to anyone. That was pretty intense."

She nodded. "Lovick Zabrecky was an intense individual. However, as I told you, he has not been seen for one hundred years. I fear him not."

"So, he just, like . . . disappeared?"

"Most likely he was killed, or became careless and met his fate. The sun is a constant enemy not always easily avoided. There was a rumor he was seen in Maine, but 'twas pure poppycock. However,

Darcourt is very much alive. He will most certainly try to get his paws on the book. When he returns, do not let him have it *under any circumstance*. Nor even glance upon it."

"Okay . . ."

"Blood swear!"

I raised my hand. "I blood swear I won't give Darcourt the book, or even show it to him." I put down my hand. "Hey, the guy who wrote the book, Eustace Tibbitt, was he a vampire too?"

"No, but he was in love with one. A woman named Leonora. That is a tale for another time. I must depart. I have matters to attend to."

"What kind of matters?"

She smiled so I could see her fangs. "Dinner."

"Oh."

"Attend to your studies, Thomas Marks—and I mean the vampiric kind."

She changed back into a bat and flew onto the windowsill.

"Are you going to come back again?" I asked.

"I turned you, so I am bound to watch over you. And it seems you need much watching over." She spread her wings. "I leave you with Dr. Franklin's words: 'Be at war with your vices, at peace with your neighbors, and let every day find you a better man' . . . or Vam-Wolf-Zom."

She checked for owls and hawks, then flew away into the night.

Now I definitely couldn't show the book to Darcourt. Where should I hide it? I fell asleep trying to think of a good place. Later, I'd regret not hiding it right then.

27.

Zeke! Zeke! Zeke!

The next morning, I told Zeke to meet me early at the bus stop. He didn't ask me why. He never does when I ask him to do stuff like that.

"Morning, T-Man. You want a cranberry cupcake?"

"No, thanks." I made sure no one else was around. "Zeke . . . look into my eyes."

"Okay, T-Man."

"You are relaxed . . . and calm . . ."

"I am . . . calm."

He was *already* hypnotized. It only took five seconds.

"Zeke . . . you can do jumping jacks again when you get excited. It's okay."

In a drowsy voice he said, "Jumping jacks . . . okay."

I snapped my fingers. "Awake."

He opened his eyes. "T-Man, I had an idea last night. What if our desks at school had motors on them like little cars, and we could drive from class to class?"

"That'd be awesome. Hey, do you want to come over and play Rabbit Attack! after school?"

"Excellent!

He started doing jumping jacks.

"Why are you smiling, T-Man?"

∘ ∘ ∘

When I got to school, I saw that somebody had written vwz in black Sharpie on the locker Abel and I share. It had to be Tanner Gantt. Had he come to school super early to do it? After first period, I came back to the locker to dump my English book, and I saw that someone had used a different-color Sharpie and had written an "I" and a red heart above vwz.

Now it said:

I ♥ VWZ.

It was a really well-drawn heart, so whoever did it was a good artist. After second period, I went to my locker and saw that someone had crossed out the heart.

Now it said:

I HATE VWZ!

After snack period, someone had crossed out "I Hate" and written: "s Are Awesome!"

So, now it said:

VWZS ARE AWESOME!

It looked like Zeke's handwriting. After third period, somebody had crossed out "Awesome" and wrote "Freaks!" so it said:

VWZS ARE FREAKS!

After fourth period, someone had added "ing awesome!" in handwriting that wasn't Zeke's.

So now it was:

VWZS ARE FREAKING AWESOME!

After lunch, Zeke, Annie, and I saw it had been changed to:

VWZS ARE FREAKING MONSTERS!

Zeke crossed out "Monsters" and changed it to:

VWZS ARE FREAKING FANTASTIC FRIENDS!

And that's when Principal Gonzales walked by. "Zeke! What are you doing?"

Zeke turned around and saluted. "Righting a wrong, Principal Gonzales."

"You are defacing school property."

"But somebody wrote something bad about Tom and I was making it good."

"That's not the point. Come with me, right now," said Principal Gonzales.

"That's not fair," said Annie. "Zeke was battling a hate crime."

A crowd of kids started watching.

"Tanner Gantt started it," I said. "He wrote on my locker first."

Principal Gonzales said, "Can you prove that, Mr. Marks? Did you see him do it?"

"No . . . but I know it was him."

"Sorry. I need proof."

I saw Tanner Gantt down the hall, watching and smiling. I could tell he loved that Zeke was getting in trouble.

"Come on, let's go, Zeke," said Principal Gonzales.

"What are you going to do to him?" I asked.

"Defacing school property is a suspension offense."

Zeke sort of looked like he might cry. He'd never gotten suspended before.

"Sorry, Zeke," I said.

"That's okay. . . . I'd do it again, T-Man."

"You're arresting the wrong man!" said Annie.

"I am not *arresting* anyone. Let's go, Zeke."

Annie turned to Zeke. "Don't worry, a lot of great people have gone to jail. Martin Luther King Jr., Henry Thoreau, Rosa Parks, Gandhi, Susan B. Anthony, Nelson Mandela."

"He is *not* going to jail!" said Principal Gonzales.

He started to walk Zeke down the hall, while kids lined up on either side. Annie started chanting, "Zeke! Zeke! Zeke!"

I did too. Some other kids joined in.

"Zeke! Zeke! Zeke!"

Zeke got a big smile on his face. He raised his fist up in the air. Now everybody in the hall was chanting—except Tanner Gantt.

"ZEKE! ZEKE! ZEKE!"

Sometimes bad people get away with stuff and don't get punished. It's not fair, but it happens. I wished I'd started the chant. Annie's really good at things like that.

Zeke didn't get suspended, though he did get sent home for the day. He told his mom what happened and she didn't get mad at him. She made him a cranberry sauce milkshake, and he said it was The Best Milkshake Ever.

28.

Future Me

That night, I had a dream that I wasn't a Vam-Wolf-Zom. That I'd never got bitten by Martha the bat, or Darcourt the werewolf, or that zombie. I could go outside in the sun without putting on sunscreen, dark glasses, a hat, and long sleeves. Seeing blood didn't make me thirsty. I wasn't hungry all the time and didn't want to eat raw meat. The full moon didn't make me grow hair and start howling. I didn't have fangs or semi-pointy ears. Nobody stared at me. Nobody pointed at me.

Nobody whispered behind my back. I was normal. I was just a regular kid.

And then I woke up.

I was still a Vam-Wolf-Zom.

○ ○ ○

"Today's topic is: Future Me," said Mr. Kessler. "What do you want to do or be when you're older? Let's go around the room."

"I'm going to be a singer and write books," said Annie.

Duh.

"I am going to be a famous artist," said Capri.

I was counting on that. I had two of her pictures and I hoped they'd be worth a lot of money someday.

Abel said, "At the moment I am focusing on something in the financial sector . . . or baking."

I'd let Abel invest my money. I'd also go to his bakery.

"I haven't decided, yet," said Zeke. "Either make roller coasters or design video games or be President of the United States."

"I want to be a teacher, like you, Mr. Kessler," said Maren Nesmith.

What a kiss-up.

"Did you want to be a teacher when you were our age, Mr. Kessler?" asked Annie.

"No. I wanted to be a lumberjack."

That was weird.

Tanner Gantt was next. What was he going to say? Thief? Hit man? Paid assassin? What did bullies grow up to be?

"Pro wrestler," he said.

That made perfect sense. He was big, he was strong, he was mean, and he liked to pick people up and throw them. He'd probably be a good wrestler. He might even get rich and famous. If that happens, I am going to be *really* mad.

"Tom, how about you?" asked Mr. Kessler.

Everybody turned around to look at me. Before I became a Vam-Wolf-Zom, they wouldn't have cared. The pressure was on.

I thought about all the different jobs I wanted to do when I was little.

THINGS I WANTED TO BE WHEN I WAS A KID

Cowboy

Firefighter

Ice Cream Truck Driver

Jedi Knight

Police Officer

Wizard

Donut Maker

Batman

Astronaut

Person Who Rides That Thing Around the Ice
Rink to Make the Ice Smooth

But who would hire a Vam-Wolf-Zom?

"I don't know what I want to be yet, Mr. Kessler," I said.

"You should be a spy, T-Man," said Zeke.

Some kids laughed, but Zeke might be right this time. Maybe I could do that.

"Hello, I'm Tom Marks. I'm here to interview for the spy job."

"Have a seat. So, what makes you think you would be a good spy?"

"I'm super strong, I have night vision and incredible hearing, and I can hypnotize people."

"Outstanding! Now, you do know that spying is dangerous work and you could be killed?"

"I do. But I can only be killed by a silver bullet or by getting beheaded or by a stake through my heart."

"Interesting. Now, there are some perks. You get to use awesome weapons. You get to drive very expensive, fast cars loaded with cool gadgets. And last, but not least, you meet dozens of beautiful, strong, intelligent, empowered women from around the world, who usually try to kill you at first, but then they end up falling in love with you."

"That sounds really—Oh, wait, I just remembered something. Twice a month my

body gets covered with hair when there's a full moon."

"Hmm? I suppose you could have those two nights off."

"And I can also turn into a bat and smoke or mist or fog."

(Hopefully, I'll be able to do that by then.)

"Excuse me, Mr. Marks. I'm confused. Are you a magician?"

"No. I'm a Vam-Wolf-Zom."

"Oh! So, you're the Vam-Wolf-Zom. Well, I am terribly sorry, but we can't hire Vam-Wolf-Zoms. Goodbye."

"Wait a minute. My friend, Annie, told me that you can't legally do that."

"What . . . ? Do you mean Chief Justice Annie Delapeña Barstow of the Supreme Court?"

"Yes. She told me that there is a federal law that says you can't discriminate, when hiring, according to race, gender, religion, origin, or disability."

"That is true, Mr. Marks. But it doesn't say anything about vampires or werewolves or zombies. We hired a vampire once. He eliminated a lot of enemy spies, but the next

day they'd turn into enemy vampire spies.
We tried a werewolf, but he ate the janitor,
who was very nice and a good janitor. And
zombies? Forget it. You try to make a spy out
of someone who moves two miles an hour
and just says 'Urgh'! But, thank you for com-
ing in, Mr. Marks."

I'd have to think of another job.

29.

Something Wicked This Way Comes

Ladies and gentlemen," announced Mr. Stock-dale, "our choir will be singing in the Winter Celebration Program. It's on Friday, December twenty-first, which means we have little time to achieve perfection."

I raised my hand.

"Mr. Stockdale, that's a full moon night."

"And your point is, Mr. Marks?"

"I'll be a werewolf."

He rolled his wheelchair over to where I was sitting. "Is that a problem?"

"Well, I'll look like a werewolf."

"You won't *look* like a werewolf," said Maren Nesmith, "you'll *be* a werewolf."

Only my family, the members of Conundrum, the mayor, Principal Gonzales, Martha Livingston, and Darcourt had seen me as a werewolf. Some of the kids looked nervous and some looked excited.

Everyone started talking.

"Tom should dress up as a reindeer since he'll be covered in fur.

"He could be the Abominable Snow Monster if we dyed his fur white."

"Or we can dye his fur green and he'll be the Grinch."

"We will decide on costumes later," said Mr. Stockdale. "We'll be singing a medley of holiday songs: Christmas, Hanukkah, Kwanzaa, Bodhi Day, and Solstice as well as a song called "Winter Is Cool."

We practiced our medley every day in class.

While we sang, Mr. Stockdale would shout stuff at us.

"Tom, stop looking at Annie! Smile, Elliot, you're having fun! Put away your phone, Esperanza! Capri, stop looking at Tom! I hope you are scratching your nose and not picking it, Landon! Sing out, Louise!"

156

The good news was I got to stand next to Annie and sing a solo in "Feliz Navidad." The bad news was everybody had to dress up in costumes. I had to wear a snowman suit. Dog Hots was a gingerbread man and was not happy. Zeke was a giant dreidel and loved it. Capri was a snowflake, Annie was an elf, Abel was a toy soldier, and Maren Nesmith was an ear of corn.

◦ ◦ ◦

The night of the concert, Mom took me to school to drop me off. The full moon had risen, so I'd already turned into a werewolf. It was the seventh time I'd turned into a werewolf, but I still hadn't gotten used to it. I wished I'd asked Darcourt more questions. I half-hoped I'd see him again and half-hoped I wouldn't, because he'd want to look at *A Vampiric Education*.

I wore the bottom half of my snowman costume and the gloves. I'd keep the head off until the concert started.

"Break a leg," said Mom, when I got out of the car. That's what you're supposed to say to someone doing a show. You can't say "good luck" because something bad will happen. It makes absolutely no sense.

I think it's weird going to school at night. It seems like a totally different place. It's quiet, because there aren't a million kids running around. It's dark, because there are hardly any lights on, and the classroom doors are locked. It's like a scary movie. I guess that everywhere I go is like a scary movie, since I'm a Vam-Wolf-Zom.

I walked toward the auditorium. I was sort of excited to sing, since I have a different voice when I'm a werewolf. It's deeper, rougher, and louder, and it sounds awesome. Nobody at school had heard it, except the band.

But I was nervous about what people would do when they saw me in full werewolf mode. I'd had to give up my *Invisible Tom Plan*, where I would just stay in the background in middle school and not get noticed. Being a Vam-Wolf-Zom sort of ruined that.

I took a deep breath, opened the door, and walked in. Zeke and Annie were the first people I saw.

"Hey, guys," I said.

"Hey, T-Man."

"Hey, Tom.

Everybody turned to look at me. I could hear what they said, even when they whispered.

"Whoa!"

"Gross."

"Check out that hair."

"Awesome."

"Ewww."

"He looks like my dog."

"He is so hairy."

"He's kind of a cute werewolf."

"I am not going anywhere near him."

"He looks like Chewbacca."

Some people wanted to touch my fur. Why not? I'd want to if I were them. When a few of the girls did it, Capri gave them weird looks. I have no idea why.

Mr. Stockdale wheeled up to me and said, "Tom, we have a problem."

Was he not going to let me be in the concert because of how I looked?

"The stage crew is late and they didn't put the piano up on stage. Can you do it?"

"Oh. Yeah. Sure."

I picked up the piano, which was easy. As I set it down, the stage crew walked in. Tanner Gantt was with them.

"What is *he* doing here?" said Annie.

"Plotting evil," said Zeke.

"I guess he's on the stage crew," said Dog Hots.

Tanner Gantt was smiling, which always means something bad is going to happen.

o o o

Backstage, I got in my snowman costume and Zeke zipped up the back.

"All set, T-Man—I mean, S-Man!"

Mr. Stockdale put white makeup on my face so I'd look more like a snowman, and we stuck on a carrot nose. There were a million people getting ready—the orchestra, the singers, the dancers. We all waited in the big dressing room, watching the show on monitors before it was our turn.

Some girls did a ballet called "The Waltz of the Snowflakes." It should have been called "The Dance That Went on Forever and Was Incredibly Boring Until One of the Snowflakes Tripped and Knocked Over Three Other Snowflakes and the Main Snowflake Yelled at Everybody."

The drama kids did a skit about a Christmas store window display that came alive. It was pretty funny. Elves went on strike at the North Pole, and Santa and Mrs. Claus had to make the toys. Zeke said we should try out for the school play in March. I said, "No, we shouldn't."

Then it was our turn for the medley. Annie and I were next to each other on the top step of the riser. Just before my solo, she whispered to me,

"Remember, don't howl." I nodded. When I'm a werewolf it's hard to not howl while singing.

We got to my solo and I sang in my rock-and-roll-werewolf voice.

"Whoa!"

"Check out Marks's voice!"

"He sounds awesome!"

The audience started clapping and cheering. Mr. Stockdale gave me a thumbs-up. It was pretty great.

For about five seconds.

I sensed that someone was standing behind me. I couldn't turn around because I was singing, but I felt a hand put something down the neck of my costume. It was about the size of a golf ball and it rolled down my back and landed with a thud in the left foot of my costume. I smelled it right away.

Garlic.

A vampire's least favorite vegetable.

30.

The Most Embarrassing Thing That Ever Happened to a Kid

My eyes started to water, I got sick to my stomach, and my muscles ached. Somebody, whose name I would bet a million dollars was spelled T-a-n-n-e-r G-a-n-t-t had slipped a garlic bulb into my costume.

Since the zipper was on the back of my stupid costume and I had giant mittens on, I couldn't unzip it and get the garlic out. I felt like I was going to faint.

I had to get out of there, get the costume off, and get rid of the garlic.

But I couldn't run because of the big snowman suit. I started to wobble down the riser. I pushed Dog Hots the gingerbread man out of the way, knocked over Zeke the giant dreidel, and banged into Maren the corn.

Mr. Stockdale gave me a I Am Going to Kill You after This Concert look.

I tried to say "Garlic!", but my tongue was swollen and I couldn't get it out.

I tripped over Capri's big elf shoes and knocked over the Christmas tree, which knocked over the giant menorah. I jumped off the stage into the audience.

Some people thought it was part of the concert and clapped.

Little kids started yelling:

"Mr. Snowman is going to kill me!"

"I don't like this show!"

"Bye, Frosty! See you next year!"

I ran up the aisle as fast as I could and banged open the back doors of the auditorium. When I got outside, I ripped off the snowman costume and threw it as far away as I could. I saw it land a football-field's length away at the other end of the parking lot.

I sucked in the clean, cold, fresh air.

Dad came out of the auditorium. "You okay, Tom?"

"Yeah," I said, catching my breath.

"What happened?"

"Somebody put garlic in my costume. I'm sure it was Tanner Gantt. But I can't prove it."

Dad held up his phone. "We might be able to. I filmed it."

This would get Tanner Gantt suspended, or maybe even expelled. This could be the beginning of the best Christmas ever!

We watched the video, but you couldn't see who was behind me. It was too dark.

Once again, Tanner Gantt got away with something.

o o o

I knew that kids would make fun of me for the rest of my life for what happened. Mom, Dad, Emma, and I all rode home together.

"It wasn't *that* bad," said Emma, who was, maybe for the first time in her life, trying to make me feel better.

"Yes, it was!" I said. "It was The Most Embarrassing Thing to Ever Happen to a Kid."

"Oh, I don't know about that," said Dad. "I think I would win The Most Embarrassing Kid Moment."

"What happened to you?" asked Emma, leaning forward in her seat. She *loves* to hear stories about bad things happening to other people.

"When I was in third grade I played Abraham Lincoln in a play. I got to say his Gettysburg Address to the whole school. I had to go to the bathroom before I went on, but I decided I could wait. Then, one of the kids forgot their lines, so we had to start over from the beginning.

"Finally, I was giving the speech. It was going well. Right around when I said, 'The world will little note, nor long remember what we say here' . . . I peed in my pants."

"YES!" said Emma.

"*But* . . . I didn't stop giving the speech. 'The show must go on.' I kept talking, and with great dignity, took off my tall, stove-pipe hat and put it in front of the wet spot on my pants. I finished the speech. People were laughing so hard they were crying; they were literally falling out of their seats. Thank goodness there was no videotaping back then."

"I would pay a *million dollars* for a video of that," said Emma. "Were there any photos?"

"My father took one picture," said Dad. "But it was 'accidentally' destroyed in a mysterious small fire in our backyard."

"So what happened?" I asked.

"For about two days, everybody called me 'President Pee,' until the principal said that would get anyone suspended for a week. Meanwhile, I told my parents that we needed to change our name and move to a different country. But my mom talked me out of it."

"You win," said Emma. "Worst Kid Moment."

"You do," I agreed. I felt about fifty percent better.

Afterward, as we got out of the car and walked toward our house, I heard Mom whisper to Dad.

"Did that *really* happen to you?"

Dad just smiled.

°°°

When we went in the house, Emma said, "Why didn't you just turn into a bat and fly out of the snowman suit?"

I gave her a dirty look for the millionth time.

"What . . . ?" said Mom.

"Tom, can you turn into a bat and fly?" said Dad.

"Yes, he can. The bat's out of the bag," said Emma, laughing at her own lame joke.

I showed Mom and Dad how I could turn into a bat and flew around the living room. Their reactions were pretty big, but not as big as when I turned into a werewolf the first time. I guess they're getting used to their son doing strange things.

It's still gotta be weird to see your kid turn into a bat.

Mom said I was a "cute" bat, which I knew she would. Dad started singing the old Batman show song until Mom made him stop. They told me to be careful when I flew outside. I didn't tell them about the time the owl almost got me.

"What's it like to fly?" asked Dad.

"It's pretty awesome."

Mom got excited. "Oh my gosh, Tom!"

"What?"

"You can put up the Christmas lights!"

Mom likes to put up a million Christmas lights on our house each year. Dad usually does it. It takes him forever, he almost always falls off the ladder, he swears a lot, says he'll hire someone to do it next year, but he never does.

Now *I* had to do it.

The next night, Mom made me turn into a bat and fly up to the roof with the string of lights in my feet. I had to fasten them along the gutters and then plug them in. It took forever because I wasn't used to holding things with my talons. (Or claws, or whatever they're called. I still have to look that up.)

Emma came out to watch and laugh at me. "Go, bat boy, go!"

Afterward, Dad whispered to me, "I am so glad I

don't have to do that anymore. I owe you one. This is going to be a great Christmas."

Maybe for him. For me it was going to be one I would never ever forget.

31.

#1 Holiday

Winter break is the best. Christmas is #1 on my Top Ten Best Holidays list. Two whole weeks off from school *and* presents. I had hoped that none of my teachers would assign any homework over the break, but they did.

I decided to do all of it on the first day of vacation, to get it over with. My family was in the kitchen, finishing breakfast, and I was about to go to the dining room to start working when Mom said, "Emma, Tom, make sure you give me your Christmas lists."

"My list is simple," said Emma. "All I want is one thing: a car."

Mom and Dad both rolled their eyes.

"It would help everyone," said Emma. "I could run errands for you, take Tom places he needs to go, visit Gram, take medicine to old, sick people, and take food to poor, starving people."

She wouldn't do *any* of that stuff.

Dad looked at Emma seriously and took her hand, which usually means he's going to make a joke.

"But Emma, how can Santa Claus fit a car down the chimney?"

He said the same thing when she was ten and had asked for a horse.

"He can leave the keys under the tree and the car outside," she said.

"Oh, Emma, my dear, darling, delusional daughter, you are going to be a very disappointed girl on Christmas morning."

Emma *always* asks for ridiculous things that she never gets. You'd think she would've learned by now.

"Okay!" she said. "If you can't get me a car, I will accept a round-trip airline ticket to Paris, two weeks at a first class hotel, and a lot of money to spend while I'm there."

"That's what *I* want!" said Mom, looking at Dad.

He smiled and took Mom's hand, "My dear, darling, delusional wife, you will also be a very disappointed girl on Christmas morning."

Mom pretended to be mad. "I knew I should've married Geoffrey Bucklezerg Kane."

That was weird she said that. He was the billionaire guy who would pay a million dollars for a copy of *A Vampiric Education*.

But I had more important things to think about. Like my Christmas list.

TOM MARKS'S CHRISTMAS LIST

1. Money (I never get it because Mom says, "No money at Christmas! Gifts only!", but I figure I might as well keep asking).

2. Gift certificates (Not exactly money, but good, unless they're to a place like The Fun Store, which doesn't have anything that is fun. My mom knows the person who owns it, so she likes to go there.)

3. Cruiser Skateboard

4. Z-Play Cube video game system (The system I have now is even older than Emma's phone.)

5. IMPORTANT!!! No socks, underwear, T-shirts, pants, belts, sweaters, or any kind of clothes, except a Killer Boss-Rot T-shirt—and make sure it is the long-sleeved one because I am one-third vampire and sunlight can kill me.

6. Rabbit Attack!: Randee's Revenge video game.

7. King Moe album (The band that Tanner Gantt had a poster of in his room. I heard one of their songs and it was pretty good.)

After Dad left to go to work, Mom pulled Emma into the living room, where I was reading. Mr. Kessler gave us a free book choice to read over the break. It had to have something about wintertime in it. I chose the shortest book I could find: *A Christmas Memory* by a guy named Truman Capote. It was only seventy-three pages. Zeke was reading *A Charlie Brown Christmas*, which was only forty-eight pages, but I don't think Mr. Kessler will allow it since it's a book for little kids.

Mom was saying, "Emma, I want you to go to the mall and get that new phone that just came out."

"Oh my God!" said Emma, excited. "Finally!"

"Not for you," said Mom. "For your father, for Christmas. You have a phone."

"My phone is, like, a hundred years old!"

"It's two years old."

"It's like an antique. Every time I use my phone my friends make fun of me."

"Then you need to get some new friends," said Mom.

"I don't want to go to the mall now," whined Emma.

"Emma, you love to go to the mall. Do your Christmas shopping."

"Okay," she sighed. "I'll call Lucas on my old, beat-up, out-of-date, sad, pathetic phone right now. I hope it still works."

"Emma, can I go with you?" I asked. "I have to do my Christmas shopping."

"No."

"Why not?"

"Why do I have to always have a reason?"

"Take your brother to the mall," said Mom. "Tom, do you want me to make you a raw-liver smoothie before you go?"

Emma made her I'm Gonna Throw Up sound.

Raw-liver smoothies were one of the ways I got blood. I know it sounds gross, but if you were a vampire you'd understand.

"No, thanks, Mom. I'm good."

I'd regret saying that.

∘ ∘ ∘

Emma, Carrot Boy, and I entered the mall through the food court, which is *always* a mistake when you're a Vam-Wolf-Zom. The second we went through the door I smelled hot dogs grilling, chicken frying, pepperoni pizza, falafels, tacos, wontons, pastrami sandwiches, hamburgers sizzling, and sweet cinnamon rolls baking. I could even smell the sushi. I wanted to eat everything.

"I gotta eat something, Emma."

"No. We're going to get Dad's stupid phone first. *Then* you can eat."

I listened to her.

Why do I do that?

The mall was jammed with people. It was right before the holidays, so I knew it would be. There was a gigantic line with about a million people waiting to get the new phone.

"Tom, get in line for Dad's stupid phone," said Emma.

"*You* get in line. You're the one Mom told to get it."

"I have to do important things."

"Like what, Babe-a-la?" asked Carrot Boy.

"I have to get makeup and lotion, and check out the sale at Hannan's. C'mon, Babe-a-la."

That was their new nickname for each other. I almost puked every time they said it.

The line for the phone was so long that it stretched outside the mall to the parking lot. It was cold, so people in line had on big jackets, hats, scarves, and gloves. I just wore a T-shirt and my hoodie. The cold doesn't bother me anymore.

"Aren't you freezing, kid?" asked a man, who was dressed like he was going on an expedition to Antarctica.

"No, I'm okay."

"You're gonna catch cold."

"I have a super-rare condition that keeps me warm," I said. I didn't want to tell him I was a Vam-Wolf-Zom.

"What it's called?" he asked.

Now I had to make up a name.

"It's called . . . hot-blood-itis."

He nodded. Then he pointed at something and said, "Speaking of blood."

I looked over at a big red-and-white bus that was parked nearby, with a sign on the side:

GIVE THE GREATEST GIFT OF ALL: BLOOD.

It was a bloodmobile.

32.

Thirsty

The bus had fresh, warm, delicious blood inside. I could almost taste it. My mouth started to water.

Why didn't I have that liver smoothie before I left? I had to get out of the line and get away from that bus. But if I lost my place, I wouldn't get the phone. Mom would kill me. I called Emma and she wouldn't answer, so I texted her.

Emergency! You have to get in line for me!

No.

Why not?!

I'm busy.

Doing what?

Trying on jeans.

There's a bloodmobile parked by the line near me!

So?

I'm one-third vampire!

So?

I drink blood!

Duh.

I HAVE TO GET AWAY FROM ALL THIS BLOOD!

You are such a pain.

COME! RIGHT! NOW!

Carrot Boy and Emma *finally* showed up, carrying three shopping bags. They took my place and I ran into the mall. I went straight to the food court, to a place called Gluckstern's Deli.

"Do you have liver?!" I asked a red-haired lady with thick glasses at the counter.

"Do we have liver? Of course we have liver. Our specialty is chopped-liver sandwiches. Delicious. What kind of bread do you want?"

"No bread. I just want some raw liver."

"Raw liver? You want raw liver? Is this some kinda joke?"

"No. And could you put it in a blender with some water? And blend it like a smoothie?"

"A raw-liver smoothie? This is not funny, young man. Do you see me laughing?"

"It's not a joke! I promise! It's . . . it's for my great-grandmother. She's a hundred and one years old and she has no teeth and she loves liver, so I take her liver smoothies."

The red-haired lady crossed her hands over her chest and looked like she was going to cry.

"You are such a good boy. My grandson should be so good to me. Sit. I make it special for great-gramma. Liver smoothie."

She made it for me and gave me a hug. I ran out of the food court, went around the corner so she wouldn't see me, and gulped it down.

Ahhhh.

o o o

I went back to the phone store, where there was no line anymore. Just Emma and Carrot Boy on a bench outside.

"What happened, Emma?" I asked.

"They ran out of Dad's stupid phone!"

Carrot Boy looked up from his phone. "Hey, I found one at We Got Phones, that store near my house. They're holding it for you."

"Thanks, Babe-a-la, you are the best!" said Emma. "Okay, we'll go get it, but first we have to go see Santa."

"Cool," said Carrot Boy.

"*What?* You want to see Santa?" I said.

"Yes. I have to get a picture. Claire Devi did it. Look."

She showed us a picture on her phone of Claire sitting on Santa's lap, posing like she was a model. Emma does everything Claire Devi does.

"I'll meet you over there," I said. "I'm going to the bookstore to get a gift."

"Is it for your *girlfriend*?" said Emma.

"No!"

o o o

I'd decided to buy Annie a gift this year. I was going to buy her a book, even though she's read practically every book in the world. At the bookstore, I found a rack of books under a sign that read OUR TOP YOUNG ADULT BEST SELLERS! 50% OFF!

I looked at the front covers and read what they were about on the back. They were all about teenagers who were sick or dying of some horrible disease, or their brother or sister or best friend died, or their pet died, or there was a war going on and a lot of people died, or there was a plague, or they lived in a fantasy world with a war and disease and more people dying.

I got depressed just reading about them.

The least depressing book was *We Died to Fall in Love*. It was about two teenagers who were sick (of course), and died (as usual) just before they went on their first date. But then they started dating as ghosts, and helped other teenagers fall in love and solve mysteries. I bought it and hoped Annie hadn't read it. The guy at the store said it had just come out that day, so she probably hadn't.

"You want a coupon to get this gift wrapped for free at a stand in the mall?" he asked.

I am the Worst Gift Wrapper. I always use too much tape and paper. I wanted it to look nice, so I walked over to the gift-wrapping place. The lady there was dressed up like Mrs. Santa Claus, in a hat with a bell, a red miniskirt, and black boots. She looked up and smiled.

"Hey! It's the Zom-Vammer-Wolf kid!"

It was Tanner Gantt's mom. I hadn't seen her since the night she tried to get her son to kill me with a baseball bat. She turned to the woman whose gift she had just wrapped.

"This is one of my son's best friends."

That was one hundred percent untrue.

"Hi, Mrs. Gantt," I said.

She giggled. "Honey, don't call me Mrs. Gantt. I'm Brandi!"

"Can you wrap this, please?"

"Heck, yeah!" she said, taking the book. "Is this for your girlfriend, hon?"

It wasn't any of her business who it was for.

"No. She's just a friend."

"I dunno, it's called *We Died to Fall in Love*. This looks pretty romantic."

I shrugged. She kept talking as she wrapped it.

"Tanner has a girlfriend. Her name's Alana Candelora. She goes to your school. Gorgeous. Beautiful. He showed me a picture. She models, I think. I'm sure you know her."

Alana Candelora? I'd never heard of anybody at school named that.

"I don't know her," I said.

"You sure? I haven't met her yet. She's a cheerleader. I was a cheerleader. I could do the splits and jump super high and everything. Okay. Done!"

She handed me the wrapped book. It looked really nice.

"Thanks, Mrs.— Brandi."

"You're welcome. Hey, why don't you come by the house sometime and watch TV, play video games. We've got a dog."

Yeah. I know. He tried to eat me once.

"Tanner would love to hang out with you."

It's weird how some parents have no idea what their kids are like.

After I left the store, I looked Alana Candelora up on our school app on my phone. There wasn't anybody with that name in the school directory. I looked her up on social media. Nothing.

33.

The Big Fat Man with the Long White Beard

Emma and Carrot Boy were still waiting to get a picture with Santa, so I sat down on a bench. There were a lot of families. Most of the kids looked excited. The babies didn't know what was going on. There was a Nice Girl Elf, who took the kids up to Santa, sitting in a big chair, and a Grumpy Guy Elf taking the pictures.

Some of the kids in line looked scared. I could see why. Santa was a big guy with heavy black boots, a long beard, and a red nose going, "Ho! Ho! Ho!" in a loud voice.

In front of Emma and Carrot Boy was one little girl who looked really frightened. I could hear her whispering to her mom.

"Mommy, I don't wanna see Santa."

"But, honey, Santa needs to know what you want for Christmas."

"*You* can tell him."

"No, *you* need to tell him, Phoebe."

"I did. We wrote him a letter."

"But we need to get a picture with Santa too."

"No, we don't. We know what he looks like."

Phoebe was making some good points. If I were her parent, I would've said, "Okay, let's go." When a kid is afraid of Santa, you shouldn't force them to see him. I knew how that girl felt. Emma used to sing that song about Santa seeing you when you're sleeping and knowing when you're awake in a creepy, scary voice. It *terrified* me as a little kid. Santa was watching me twenty-four hours a day? He saw *everything* I did? I asked Mom and Dad about it, and Emma got in BIG trouble.

Phoebe started looking over at me. She tugged on her mom's sleeve and pointed.

"Mommy, look. It's the vammy-wolfie-zommy boy we saw on TV."

When I first turned into a Vam-Wolf-Zom, they

had an assembly at school and I was on TV. Phoebe must have seen it.

"Yes, it is honey," said her mom. "Don't point, that's rude."

"Mommy, I want vammy-wolfy-zommy boy to go with me to see Santa. He can protect me."

What? Why was she afraid of Santa Claus and not me? I'm a monster. Actually, I'm *three* monsters. Kids are weird. Sometimes they like monsters. Her mom waved for me to come over, so I did. She asked if I'd go with Phoebe to see Santa, and I said I would.

Carrot Boy gave me a thumbs-up. Emma was too busy putting on makeup to notice.

"If Santa attacks me, you can fight him," said Phoebe.

"He won't attack you," I said. "Santa likes you."

"My big sister said Santa attacks kids sometimes."

Her sister sounded like Emma.

"Your sister is wrong."

We went up to see Santa. Nice Elf looked at Santa and tugged on her earlobe. He nodded. That must be code for "Here comes a scared kid."

"Hello," he said. "What is your name?"

"Phoebe Amberson Welles," she said softly.

"That's a lovely name. Would you like to sit on my lap?"

She shook her head.

"That's okay. What would you like for Christmas this year, Phoebe?"

Phoebe told him she wanted some toy horse called Deewaddle Trickabee. Santa looked at Phoebe's mom, who gave him a little nod.

"I'll try to do that, Phoebe," he said.

Grumpy Elf got ready to take the picture. Phoebe pointed at Santa. "If you try to attack me, vammy-wolfy-zommy boy will get you."

Santa looked confused. Nice Elf looked excited. Grumpy Elf took the picture. Phoebe thanked me and started to walk away with her mom, and so did I, but Nice Elf grabbed my arm.

"Santa, this is the Vam-Wolf-Zom kid we were talking about . . . up at the North Pole!"

Santa's eyes got really big behind his glasses. He edged away from me in his chair. It sounded like he gulped. Was he afraid?

"Uh . . . Santa needs to go feed the reindeer now," he said.

"But we *just fed* the reindeer, Santa," said Nice Elf.

You could tell from the way they said "feeding

reindeer" it was code that meant, "I need to take a break," or "I want to get out of here," or "I have to go to the bathroom," or "This kid just peed on me, I need to change my pants," or in this case, "I don't want to talk to a Vam-Wolf-Zom!"

I think Santa was afraid of me.

"We have to get a picture!" said Nice Elf. "Here! Sit on Santa's lap!"

She shoved me onto Santa's lap, which was the last place I wanted to be. I could tell that Santa didn't want me there either. Nice Elf leaned in next to me.

"You won't see me in the picture," I explained for the millionth time. "Vampires don't show up, even on digital cameras."

"Say 'mistletoe,'" said Grumpy Elf, and he started taking pictures.

Emma was getting impatient. "He's not lying. He won't show up! It's my turn."

They didn't listen to either of us. So, there I was, in the middle of the mall, sitting on Santa Claus's lap, and who walked by?

Tanner Gantt.

When he saw me, he looked like somebody who'd just won the lottery.

"Oh, look!" he yelled. "Widdle Tommy Marks went to see Santy Claus! How adorable! What are you asking Santy for? A new doll? A toy train?"

I jumped off Santa, who seemed glad to see me go.

"Hey, I can't see the Vam-Wolf-Zom kid in the picture," said Grumpy Elf, looking at his camera screen. "He's all blurry."

"I told you!" said Emma.

Meanwhile, I had to walk right by Tanner Gantt, who was still laughing.

"That was so sweet, Marksy! I hope you've been a good widdle boy, so all your Christmas dreams come true!"

I was going to just walk away. But instead I turned around and said, "How's Alana Candelora?"

He looked surprised. "What . . . ?"

"Alana Candelora. Your girlfriend."

He pretended to be confused. "What . . . what are you talking about?"

"Alana. The beautiful cheerleader who goes to school with us. Your mom told me about her." I saw he was holding a bag from a store called

Pretty Little Things. "Is that her Christmas gift? Wait. I forgot. She isn't real, she's your pretend girlfriend that you made up."

Tanner got red in the face. "I don't know what you're talking about."

He walked away.

○ ○ ○

Emma was on Santa's lap, posing just like Claire Devi. She was hugging Santa and puffing her lips out and tossing her hair around and making stupid faces. Grumpy Elf was getting mad.

"Miss, we're not doing a fashion shoot here! Other people are waiting to get a picture!"

Emma finally got off Santa's lap. She and Carrot Boy walked over to my bench.

"I have to go the ladies' room," announced Emma. "I'll be back in a minute."

Emma takes *forever* in the bathroom. I don't know what she does in there. This time she was probably posting her pictures with Santa. Carrot Boy and I talked about that for a while, and then he looked up and asked, "Who's that with Emma?"

She was walking toward us with a tall teenager wearing track pants and a hoodie. He looked about eighteen. One of those handsome guys who was really good at any sport he tried. He was talking and smiling, and Emma was laughing like he was the funniest guy in the world. Carrot Boy got a weird expression on his face.

"I don't know," I said.

Emma and Mr. Handsome Face walked up to us. She didn't kiss Carrot Boy, like she usually does when they haven't seen each other for five minutes.

"You are so totally *not* going to believe this," she said. "I dropped my phone outside the ladies room, and this sweet guy found it and gave it back to me. How awesome is that?"

I could tell Carrot Boy didn't think it was awesome. Emma pointed at him.

"This is my friend, Lucas."

Friend?

I sniffed the air. Something smelled familiar.

"And this is my brother, Tom." She turned to Mr. Handsome Face. "This is—Oh, I'm so sorry. I don't know your name."

The guy smiled one of those perfect movie-star smiles.

"No worries. My name's Darcourt."

34.

Wolfed

Emma was talking to a werewolf and didn't know it. I hadn't recognized Darcourt, since I'd only seen him as a wolf.

He turned to me. "Hey, Mr. Vam-Wolf-Zom, how's it going?"

"It's going . . . okay," I said cautiously.

"What?" said Emma, surprised. "You two know each other?"

"Yeah," said Darcourt. "Tom and I met up about a month ago. Near your grandma's."

"What are you doing here?" I asked, even though

I knew. He wanted to see *A Vampiric Education.*

"Somebody has something special they want to show me," he said.

"Do you live nearby?" asked Carrot Boy, who didn't look very happy that Emma was practically drooling over Darcourt.

"No. I'm just passing through."

Carrot Boy looked a little less unhappy.

"Can I talk to you in private for a second?" I asked.

"Sure," said Darcourt. He turned to Emma. "Don't go anywhere. I shall return."

She giggled and said, "I won't."

Carrot Boy made a growly noise.

Darcourt and I walked over to some drinking fountains.

"Good to see you," he said.

"How'd you find me?"

He grinned. "It's not hard to find somebody, when you *really* want to find them. And I remembered your scent. That Vam-Wolf-Zom odor is one of a kind. So, how about we go back to your house so I can check out that vampire book?"

I couldn't show it to him. I had to think fast and come up with something great.

"Uh . . . actually, I don't have the book anymore."

He got serious. "Why not?"

"I gave it to Martha a couple weeks ago. She wanted it back."

"You were all done? You learned how to turn to smoke and everything?"

"Yeah, I did," I lied. I sounded pretty believable. Probably because I've been living with Emma, The Queen of Liars, and watching her lie for almost twelve years.

"Congrats. Let me see you turn to smoke."

"Uh. . . . Not here. People would think there was a fire."

"Good point. So, why did Martha want it back?"

"She's going to sell it." Why did I say that?

"Really? Selling that book is against the vamp code."

"She's selling it to raise money . . . for a charity."

"What charity?"

WHY DID HE KEEP ASKING ALL THESE QUESTIONS?!

"She's . . . she's starting a home for baby vampires."

I couldn't believe I said that. It sounded like something Zeke would say.

Darcourt looked like he was deciding whether to believe me or not.

"That sounds like something Martha would do. Is she going to have an auction? Sell it on eBay?"

Darcourt would be able to find out if that was true.

"No. . . . That famous billionaire guy, Geoffrey Bucklezerg Kane, he's going to buy it."

"Has she sold it to him yet?"

"I don't know. Maybe."

Darcourt nodded. "Good to know."

Phew. He believed me.

"I better get back to my sister. We have to get home."

We walked back to Emma and Carrot Boy.

Darcourt said, "Hey, Lucas, Emma, nice to meet you. I've gotta go."

"Right now? Really?" said Emma, like he had just told her they cancelled Christmas.

"That's too bad," said Carrot Boy, with a big smile.

Darcourt turned to me. "Later, Tom. I know I'll be seeing you again."

o o o

Emma and Carrot Boy had a fight about Darcourt, but it lasted only ten minutes. They made up on the drive to the phone store and invented new nicknames. They are so bad I'm not even going to tell you what they are. We got dad's phone and went home. I was already pretty hungry again.

"Did you get it?" asked Mom as soon as we walked in the house.

"Yes . . . I did," said Emma, putting on a tired voice and collapsing on the sofa. "It was a total nightmare. . . . I waited in line *forever*. . . . Then, they ran out of phones. . . . We drove all over the place and finally found one. . . . It was a painful, exhausting, horrible ordeal."

Mom rolled her eyes. She knew.

"Thank you, Emma. Thank you, Tom."

I vowed to never go shopping with Emma again.

Meanwhile, a horrible night was ahead of me.

35.

Have Yourself a Merry Little Murder

Gram drove down to our house on Christmas Eve morning, like she usually does.

"How's my favorite Vam-Wolf-Zom?" she said, giving me a hug.

I had already told her I could turn into a bat and fly, so it wasn't a total shock when I showed her in the living room. When I finished flying and turned back into me, she said, "Well . . . If someone had told me that one day I would watch my grandson turn into a bat and fly, I would have said . . . far out!"

Mom got me my own ham for dinner. After we did the dishes, she made one of her announcements.

"We are going to do something different this Christmas Eve."

Emma and I groaned.

Carrot Boy, who is always at our house now, was the only one who got excited. "What're we gonna do, Mrs. Marks?"

"We are going to go Christmas caroling!"

"Have fun," said Emma. "I'll be here on this sofa."

"C'mon, Emma-bemma-lemma, it'll be fun," said Carrot Boy.

This was their worst nickname ever. Even worse than the one I didn't tell you about.

"No. It won't," said Emma. "Why can't we just stay home and watch a Christmas movie? Isn't that what Christmas is all about?"

"No," said Gram.

"Well, I am not going," said Emma.

Dad stood up and said, "As you wish. But let it be known throughout the land, that if you do not go caroling, there shall be no gifts for you under the tree on Christmas morn. And your stocking shall be empty, save for one piece of black coal. And you will get no roast beast, no Who-pudding and no Who-hash. . . . And the angels will weep for you."

Mom, Gram, and I laughed. Emma didn't. Carrot Boy looked worried. I think he thought Dad was serious.

"But I don't know the stupid words to the songs!" Emma whined.

"And that is why I printed them out," said Mom, handing us pages stapled together.

We all went caroling.

o o o

The first house we went to was Professor Beiersdorfer's, the retired scientist who lives across the street. Zeke and I used to be afraid of him—when we thought he was going to turn us into robots—but not anymore.

When he opened the door, he was already in his robe, pajamas, and slippers even though it was only seven thirty. Old people do that for some reason.

"Ah, the Christmas carolers," he said. "Wunderbar!"

"What carol would you like to hear, Professor Beiersdorfer?" asked Mom.

"Could you sing 'O Tannenbaum'? It is mein favorite. Mama und Papa sang that to me when I was a kinder, long ago in Vienna."

We started singing, except for Emma, until Mom jabbed her in the ribs.

"O Christmas tree, o Christmas tree."

Professor B started singing along with us in German.

"O Tannenbaum, o Tannenbaum."

Everything was fine until he started crying a little. Then Mom got tears in her eyes. So did Dad and Gram. And so did Carrot Boy. Everybody except me and Emma was singing and crying at the same time. It didn't sound very good. Emma and I looked at each other, rolled our eyes, and kept singing. We were almost finished when Professor B got this weird expression on his face.

Mom stopped singing (and crying) and said, "Are you okay, Professor?"

He opened his mouth, but didn't say anything. His face went pale, and then he grabbed his chest with both hands and fell down in the doorway.

Were we The Christmas Carol Killers?

36.

The Hundred-Year-Old Man

Mom called 911 and an ambulance took Professor B to the hospital. Dad went with him. I've always wanted to ride in an ambulance and speed through red lights, but I didn't ask. The rest of us got in our car and went to the hospital. Emma didn't want to go. Mom made her.

Luckily, Professor B was okay. The doctor said he'd had a mild heart attack because he'd forgotten to take some pills. He'd be able to go home tomorrow. When we visited him in his room, he

thanked us, even though we were sort of respon-
sible for him being there.

We were walking toward the elevator to go
home when Mom stopped, grabbed Dad's arm,
and said, "I've got a great idea!"

"No, you don't," said Emma. "We are going to
go home and go to sleep and try to salvage The
Christmas That Is Being Ruined."

"We should sing to some of the patients here,"
said Mom. "Think how much they would love
that!"

Emma freaked. "Mom, this isn't *The Sound of
Music*. We're not the Trapp Family Singers."

"I'll ask the nurse if it's okay," said Gram.

"Did you guys forget that we almost *killed* somebody with our caroling?" said Emma.

"Someone doesn't have the Christmas spirit,"
said Dad.

"No," said Emma. "I don't."

Gram came back and said the nurse told her it
was okay.

We went into the first room and sang to a man
who looked a hundred years old. Emma was sulky
until he looked up at her and said, "You are the
most beautiful girl I have ever seen in my life. You
look like an angel."

Then, of course, she loved him. She made us sing him two songs.

A nurse came in during my solo on "Silent Night," which bugged me. She could have waited until I was done, but she started checking the machines that were hooked up to the Hundred-Year-Old Man.

"Keep singing, it's lovely, don't mind me," she said, as she took out a plastic vial and a needle and started taking his blood and putting it in the vial. I wanted to say, *"Please don't do that now. I'm one-third vampire."* She pulled out another vial and took *more* blood. And then another. The Hundred-Year-Old Man wasn't going to have any more blood inside him. It was as bad as the bloodmobile. I felt like the blood in the vials was saying, *"Drink me! Drink me!"*

"I gotta go!" I said, running to the door. "Meet you at the car!"

"What's the matter?" asked Mom.

"I'm a vampire," I reminded her. "Blood!"

"Oh, right! Sorry! I forgot."

How do you forget your son is a Vam-Wolf-Zom?

I heard them singing as I ran down the hall. Emma took over my solo, which also bugged me, because she's not a very good singer. I took the elevator and another nurse got on with a tray filled with more tubes of fresh, warm, tasty blood. I jumped out of the elevator just before the doors closed and ran down the stairs.

Who knew hospitals were so dangerous?

Finally, my family came out to the car and we drove home. Dad yawned and looked at his watch.

"Merry Christmas."

"Merry Christmas," said Mom.

"Merry Christmas," said Gram.

"Merry Christmas," said Carrot Boy.

"If anybody wakes me up before noon they will suffer the consequences," said Emma.

"Everybody sleep in," said Mom. "No need to get up early. We'll have a late Christmas."

"And to all a good night," said Carrot Boy.

37.

The Best Worst Day of the Year

Waking up on Christmas morning might be the best part of the day. You haven't opened your gifts yet, so you can lie in bed and imagine and wonder and guess what's under the tree. It could be *anything*.

I woke up early. Everybody else was sleeping in because we'd been up late the night before. I got out of bed and went to the window. It had snowed overnight. Trees, sidewalks, and front lawns were covered with fresh, white, powdery snow.

I opened my window and took a deep breath. I could smell the fresh, cold air, people making coffee, bacon frying, and wood burning in people's fireplaces. I heard some bells ringing in the distance.

It was a *perfect* Christmas morning.

And then I saw it.

The snowman.

Except it wasn't a man exactly.

It had hairy hands with claws, slicked-back hair, furry ears, fangs with blood painted on them, a long furry tail, a Santa hat, and a human arm sticking out of its mouth.

It was a Vam-Wolf-Zom snowman.

It was me.

In front of it, someone had spray-painted SCARY CHRISTMAS! in the snow.

I have to admit, it was pretty awesome looking. If there were a Snowman Contest, it would win first place. Tanner Gantt must have made it in the middle of the night. I bet it took him a long time.

I got dressed and went outside to take it down. I knew if Mom and Dad saw it they'd get mad. I didn't want it to ruin Christmas. I did take a picture with my phone first, just in case I needed it as evidence.

Then, I decided to pay Tanner Gantt a visit.

As I walked over, I made a list in my mind.

THINGS TO DO TO TANNER GANTT

1. Make a snowman that looked like Tanner Gantt on his front lawn. (But that would be a lot of work and I'm not a good artist, so it wouldn't look like him. Capri could make an awesome one, but she'd probably get mad if I woke her up early on Christmas morning.)

2. Show Tanner's mother the picture of the snowman and have her punish him. (I didn't know what she'd do. Maybe

nothing, or maybe something really bad. I couldn't trust her.)

3. Tell Tanner Gantt my parents had called the police and he was going to be arrested and spend Christmas Day in jail. (I liked that one.)

When I walked up to his house, I saw the curtains were closed in the living room window, but I could tell there was a light on. I peeked in through a small space between the curtains.

Tanner Gantt was sitting on the sofa watching *A Charlie Brown Christmas*. That was the last thing I thought he'd be watching. I bet a lot of people watch things you'd be surprised they watch, when they're alone. There was a small Christmas tree in the corner of the room with some gifts under it.

I was all set to knock on his door and yell at him when I had an idea.

Tanner Gantt obviously wanted me to see the snowman, get mad, and yell at him. He wanted a big reaction after all the work he'd done in the middle of the night.

But what if I didn't do what he expected? That might bug him even more.

I knocked on the front door and heard him

turn off the TV. He peeked out the peephole, then opened the door. You could tell he was waiting for me to say something about the snowman by the smirk on his face.

"What do you want, Marks?"

"I just came over to say Merry Christmas."

I said it like I really meant it, all friendly, with a smile. He was confused.

"What . . . ?"

"Merry Christmas!"

I didn't say anything about the snowman. I could tell he was waiting for me to say something.

"Did you look on your front lawn this morning?" he asked.

"Yeah."

"Did you see anything?"

"No."

"You *didn't*?" He looked surprised.

"No."

He believed me. I'm a pretty good actor sometimes. Maybe Zeke is right and I should try out for the school play.

Tanner looked mad, probably because he'd gotten up in the middle of the night to make that snowman.

"You seriously didn't see the snowman on your front lawn?!"

"Ohhhhh," I said. "Yeah. The snowman that looked like me." I laughed. "That was pretty funny. You did an awesome job."

His jaw dropped. I just kept talking.

"So, did you have a good Christmas? You get any awesome gifts? We haven't opened ours yet. Did you watch any special Christmas shows? My favorite is *Charlie Brown*. Do you wanna build a snowman?"

Tanner Gantt said the worst thing that you can say to a person.

I just smiled and said, "Merry Christmas!"

He slammed the door in my face.

I walked away, humming "Jingle Bells."

o o o

I was going to leave, but I wanted to see what he'd do next. I peeked through the space between the curtains again. He was back on the sofa.

"Mom!" he yelled. "When're we gonna open gifts?"

"Okay, okay!" she yelled, from somewhere. "I'm coming!"

Mrs. Gantt walked in wearing a robe and carrying a giant cup of coffee. She looked different with no makeup and her hair just messy. She picked up a box with a red ribbon around it, from under the tree.

"Merry Christmas, Tanner."

He took the box, shook it a little to test the weight, to see if he could tell what it was. I do that too. He unwrapped it. It was a green jacket, with a hood and these special orange zippers. Kids used to wear them, like three years ago. I had one. So did Zeke and Dog Hots.

I could tell he didn't like it. "Why'd you get me *this*?"

"It's cool. Lotsa kids wear these."

"Not anymore. Nobody wears these." That was true. We never wore ours anymore. He threw it back in the box.

"I didn't want a stupid jacket. I wanted the Z-Play Cube game system. I told you."

"I know. . . . But I couldn't get that."

"Why not?"

"Because we're not rich, Tanner. Your dad's late with his check, *again*, and that job at the mall paid like nothing . . . and . . . and other stuff."

"What other stuff?"

"Never mind . . ."

She started crying. He just stood there for a while. Then, he took the jacket back out of the box and put it on.

"It's not that bad," he said.

She wiped her eyes.

"Next year'll be better, Tanner. . . . I promise."

He gave her a gift. It was a necklace. That's what must have been in the Pretty Little Things bag at the mall. She started crying again, but it was a different kind of crying. "You want me to make some Christmas pancakes, like I used to?" she asked.

"Sure. . . . Is Dad coming over?"

"No. He texted me last night. I forgot to tell you."

Tanner Gantt turned the TV on again and they started watching *Charlie Brown*. Now I felt bad again. I wished I hadn't gone back to look. I have to stop spying on people.

38.

Surprise Visitors

When I got home, Gram had just woken up. "Hey! It's Christmas!" she shouted from the top of the stairs. "Let's get this show on the road!"

Mom dragged Emma out of her room, Gram made coffee, and Dad put on Christmas music. We had just started to open our gifts when the doorbell rang. Dad opened the door. It was Carrot Boy, in his robe and pajamas, holding a bunch of gifts.

"Merry Christmas, Mr. Marks! Is it too early?"

Dad yawned. "Yes. It is. But come on in."

"Don't let him in!" screamed Emma, as she ran upstairs. She didn't want Carrot Boy to see her until she'd put on makeup and done her hair. I think Emma actually looks better without all the makeup and junk she puts in her hair. I tried to tell her that once. It did not go well.

We finally opened our gifts after she came back down.

I got the Z-Play Cube game system and the new Rabbit Attack! video game, and Gram gave me a subscription to a thing called Meat of the Month Club.

Emma gave me a new skateboard. It was the first good gift she'd ever given me. I bet Carrot Boy made her do it and chipped in to pay for it.

Gram is a big horror-movie fan and I made her a great gift. I bought three different action figures—a vampire, a werewolf, and zombie—took them apart and mashed them up together to make a Vam-Wolf-Zom. She loved it.

I gave Carrot Boy a gift certificate to Taco! Taco! Taco!, his favorite place to eat.

Carrot Boy gave Emma some clothes, and she had to try them all on and do a boring fashion show for us. She gave him a big, framed photograph of herself. At least she hadn't painted a self-portrait. I was glad they did not give each other new nicknames.

Mom gave Dad his phone, which he loved. Emma started to tell him how unbelievably hard it was to get, but Mom made her stop. As a joke, Dad gave Emma a little toy car. She didn't think it was funny and threw it away.

I kept thinking about Tanner Gantt's Christmas. I may be a Vam-Wolf-Zom, but I'd rather be me than him.

◦ ◦ ◦

That afternoon, somebody I didn't expect to see on Christmas showed up.

"One of your girlfriends is here," said Emma, looking out the window.

Capri, wearing a Santa hat, was walking up to our house holding a gift.

"She's not my girlfriend, Emma!"

"You'd better tell her that," said Emma, as she went upstairs.

I opened the front door.

"Merry Christmas, Tom."

"Oh. Hey, Capri." I pointed at the gift. "What's that?"

"It's a Christmas gift, Dorkus Magee."

Why did Capri get me a gift? Now I had to give *her* one. Those are The Christmas Rules.

"Aren't you going to open it?" she said impatiently.

"Oh, yeah." It was a painting of Capri looking out a window. Now I had three pictures by Capri. If she did become famous someday, I could be rich.

"Thanks, Capri."

She was looking at me with a Where Is My Gift? expression.

I said, "Um . . . your gift is upstairs."

She acted surprised. "Oh, *really*? You got me something? You didn't have to do that. That is so sweet."

"I'll be right back."

I ran upstairs and knocked on Emma's door.

"I am not receiving visitors!" she yelled.

"Emma, I need a gift for Capri."

"I am not a store!"

"Come on! Please!"

She opened her door.

"So, she *is* your girlfriend."

"She's not. Do you have something I can give her?"

She picked up a bottle of perfume. "Here. Take this."

I got suspicious. "What's wrong with it?"

"Karl Kreese gave it to me."

He was one of Emma's old boyfriends. She used to love him, but now she hated him. I tossed the bottle in a gift bag, ran downstairs, and gave it to Capri.

"Thank you, Tom! I love perfume! This is so sweet."

It was just a bottle of perfume.

"And it's called Love Dreams," she said in a weird voice.

Love Dreams?! I didn't see that. Why did they have to name it that?

She put some on her wrist and smelled it.

"Mmm. Doesn't that smell amazing, Tom?"

She stuck her wrist in my face. It was like she'd shoved a million roses and a truckload of lemons up my nose. That's the problem with having a super sense of smell. She put more perfume on her neck, and I felt like I might puke.

Capri smiled. "Every time I put it on . . . I'll think of you."

She gave me a hug. I held my breath so I wouldn't throw up.

"Merry Christmas, Tom!"

She skipped away down the sidewalk.

I took Annie's gift over to her house later that afternoon.

"Merry Christmas, Annie."

I could tell she was surprised to see me as soon as she opened the door. It was probably the same way I looked when Capri showed up.

"Oh. . . . Uh. . . . Hi, Tom. Merry Christmas. Is that for me?"

"Yeah."

"I didn't know we were exchanging gifts."

"We're not—well, I mean—I just saw this and thought you'd like it. I didn't spend very much. It was on sale."

Why did I say that?

"Come on in," she said. Her house smelled amazing.

"What smells so good?"

"We made tamales. It's one of our Christmas traditions. Do you want one?"

"Can I have five?"

She laughed, but I wasn't joking. She unwrapped the book.

"*We Died to Fall in Love.* . . . Oh . . . I haven't heard of this. Thanks, Tom."

She didn't sound too excited. I should have given *her* the perfume and Capri the book.

"You should inscribe it. I'll get a pen."

Inscribe it? I'd never inscribed a book before. I didn't know what to write.

Annie came back with a pen.

I wrote,

To Annie

Now what?

You love books, so I got you one.

That may be one of the dumbest inscriptions ever. How should I sign it?

Love?

No!

Yours truly? Sincerely? Best wishes?

It wasn't a letter!

Why is there so much pressure at Christmas? It's exhausting. I finally signed it:

Merry Christmas, Tom

Annie said, "I'm sorry, I didn't get you a gift. But I do have something I want to give you. I'll be right back."

I stood there wondering what she was going to give me.

A new song about me that was *not* about me spying on her?

A poem about me?

A picture of herself signed "*To Tom, the coolest person I know. Love, Annie.*"

It wasn't any of those things.

She came back holding a book with a ribbon tied around it.

"I hope you like it. . . . And I hope it doesn't bring back any bad diorama memories."

It was *Poems of Emily Dickinson*, the book she'd been reading on the bus. It looked like it was a million pages long and had an old black-and-white picture of Emily on the cover. She looked sort of pretty and sort of scary and sort of sad all at the same time.

"Thanks, Annie."

"Call me as soon as you finish, so we can talk about it."

It would take forever to read this. I wouldn't be calling her for a year.

"Annie!" called her mom. "Time to get dressed, we're leaving."

"Okay, Mom! I gotta go, Tom. We're going to mi abuelita's. Thanks for the book."

She gave me a hug. I think it was about two seconds longer than the one Capri gave me. On the way home, I opened the book to see if she had written in it.

"*To Tom,*

Here are some wonderful poems for a wonderful friend.

¡Feliz Navidad!

Annie."

Wonderful friend?

I *definitely* should have given her the perfume.

39.

At Long Last

On New Year's Eve, Zeke spent the night. We tried to stay up until midnight, watching movies in the living room. But Zeke fell asleep about ten-thirty and I fell asleep soon after that. We woke up at midnight when we heard firecrackers and horns and people yelling around the neighborhood. We said, "Happy New Year!" to each other and went back to sleep. New Year's Eve always feels like you're forcing yourself to stay up late and have fun, and then you just end up tired the whole next day.

I made a New Year's resolution list.

TOM'S NEW YEAR'S RESOLUTIONS

1. Come up with a billion dollar idea
2. Read the Emily Dickinson book Annie gave me.
3. Do homework **EARLY** not the night before it is due
4. Avoid Tanner Gantt **OR** be super nice to confuse him.
5. Win the school talent show
6. Learn how to transform into **SMOKE!**
7. Hide "A Vampiric Education" in a new, better, secret place.

Winter vacation went by way too fast. Back at school, Tanner Gantt pretty much ignored me. He was hanging out with a tough-looking eighth grader named Ross Bagdasarian and a skinny, scary-looking seventh grader named Gary Nathanson. They were probably starting a gang.

I kept trying to transform into smoke, every night without any luck. I practiced hypnotizing too, but smoke transformation was my #1 goal. I read over the instructions for the millionth time.

Transforming to Smoke, Fog, or Mist

If you wish to turn to smoke, fog, or mist, take heed. Picture your body as smoke. Repeat this incantation, silently: "To smoke (or mist or fog) become, become smoke (or mist or fog)." Repeat until you achieve the desired effect. To return to your human state, repeat: "To human return, return to human." Concentrate and focus all your mind upon this task. Let no other thought cross your mind.

That was *really* hard to do. I kept thinking about other stuff, like my birthday coming up, Annie's hair, Conundrum's chances of winning the talent show, Tanner Gantt, Vacuum Girl, if Darcourt was going to come back, Martha Livingston's green eyes, and the zombie that bit me.

When the gas station where I found him burned down, did he escape? I saw footprints going out into the woods when I went back there. Was he wandering around somewhere? Did he get killed? Did he end up in some other carnival? Would I ever see him again?

It was hard to concentrate on turning to smoke with all these things going on in my head.

◦ ◦ ◦

The next day at school, I'd totally forgotten about an English test we were having. But I had an idea. I was going to try something I'd *never* done before. I got to class early and went up to Mr. Kessler at his desk. A few kids came in and sat down at their desks, so I talked quietly.

"Mr. Kessler?"

"What can I do for you, Marks?"

"*Look* in my eyes."

"Is there a problem?"

"Yeah, I think I've got something in them."

He leaned in closer.

"I don't see anything."

"Look . . . closer." I stared as hard as I could. "We don't need to take that test today."

He replied in a sleepy voice, "Don't . . . need . . . to take test."

"We can take it tomorrow."

"Take . . . tomorrow."

"Today we can do whatever we want."

"Do . . . whatever . . . you want."

I snapped my fingers and sat down at my desk. Then bell rang and Mr. Kessler said, "Okay, listen up, people. Do whatever you want today."

It worked! This was a major game changer.

Then, Maren Nesmith raised her stupid hand.

"But Mr. Kessler, we have a test today on chapters fourteen through twenty."

"No, Maren. . . . Do whatever you want today."

She pointed at the board. "But you wrote it on the board."

He turned and looked at the board behind him. "What? . . . Oh . . . yeah. . . . You're right. We do have a test. Thanks, Maren."

Next time I needed to hypnotize *Maren* first.

After class, Annie and I were walking down the hall.

"You hypnotized Kessler, didn't you?"

I could tell from her voice that she didn't approve.

"Yeah. I just wanted to see if I could do it."

"Well, remember: With great power—"

"Comes great responsibility. I know."

Then, she grabbed my arm and gave me a super-serious look. "Don't *ever* try to hypnotize me."

o o o

That night, after trying a million times, I was ready to give up on transforming to smoke. Zeke came over to try to help.

"Maybe you're trying too hard, T-Man? Why

don't you just not think about it, like you don't even care."

It was worth a try. I said, "To smoke become, become smoke."

Poof! I turned into smoke.

"T-Man, you're smoke!"

I felt super light and floaty. To move, I sort of leaned in one direction. I floated across the room and went through the crack under my window. Floating outside, I saw Emma in her bedroom.

She had pulled out her old ukulele, which she only knew two chords on, and was singing a song that she wrote called "I Love My Little Luca."

I only heard one verse, but it was The Worst Song Ever Written. I didn't stay to listen or watch. I had a new No Spying Rule. I went back through the window crack into my room.

"See if you can go through me!" said Zeke.

I floated right through him.

"Excellent!"

"Did you feel me going through?"

"Just a bit. Hey, can you move stuff?"

I pushed my chair and it moved across the room. Zeke started doing jumping jacks.

"You are The Smoke-Man!"

I had mastered two skills: hypnotism and smoke transformation. Soon enough, I'd need to use them both.

40.

May the Best Act Win

SHOW US YOUR TALENT!
Hamilton Middle School Talent Show

Prizes! Fun!
Auditions: January 6th 3:30 PM in Auditorium

Show: January 12th 7:00 PM

Grand Prize
Winning Act goes to
Hollywood Hamburger Hang Restaurant!

"What song shall we be playing for the audition?" asked Abel, as we set up to practice at Annie's house.

"We'll do 'Spying,'" said Annie. "That's our best song."

I didn't want to do that for two reasons.

1. I only sang on the chorus.

2. It was about me spying on her.

"I don't think that's our best song," I said. "What about 'Table of Shame'?"

Annie wrote a great song about the time we had Silent Lunch.

"I don't care what song we do as long as I have a drum solo," said Dog Hots.

Annie glared at him. "There is no drum solo in 'Spying.'"

"Then, I don't want to do it."

Zeke jumped up. "Guys, we need to have a smoke machine and fireworks and lasers for the talent contest!"

"The school won't allow that," said Annie. "Besides, it's about the music. We don't need special effects."

"Okay. . . . What about if I run across the stage with a sparkler?"

"No, Zeke."

"A flashlight?"

"No!"

"A streamer?"

"NO!"

Capri, who was playing the same two notes over and over at the piano, didn't say anything. But it looked like she wanted to.

We practiced "Spying" for the next two weeks. I have to admit, it sounded pretty good, even though I only got to harmonize on the chorus. The Talent Show would be our very first performance, but Conundrum had a chance of winning. Unless something crazy happened.

○ ○ ○

Three days before the audition, we were just about to do "Spying" for the millionth time. Annie's mom was making nachos for us in the kitchen. They smelled delicious and I was zombie-hungry as usual.

Annie counted off. "One, two, three—"

Capri held up her hand. "Wait. Guys, I think we should do a different song."

Annie looked at her like she'd suggested we do a trampoline act instead.

"A *different* song? Why?"

"Look, we want to win this, right? The judges are Principal Gonzales and two teachers. If we do a song they like, we'll win."

"She has a point," said Dog Hots, scratching his head with a drumstick.

"What is the song you are suggesting for consideration?" asked Abel.

Capri smiled. "It's called 'School Is Cool'."

Annie made a sound like she was puking.

Capri went on. "The judges will love it and we'll win."

"Can I do a drum solo?" asked Dog Hots.

Capri nodded. "It'd be awesome with a drum solo."

"I'm in!" said Dog Hots.

Annie held up her hand. "Hold it! I've never even heard of that song."

"I know. I just wrote it today," said Capri, proudly, as she held up a piece of notebook paper. "It's awesome!"

"You've never written a song before," said Annie.

"It was super easy. I wrote it in, like, five minutes."

"You can't write a good song in five minutes."

"But I did," said Capri.

Annie was not a happy camper. "I am not doing a song called 'School Is Cool.'"

Abel cleared his throat. "I propose that we hear Capri's song, have a discussion of its pros and cons, and then make an informed decision."

Annie sat down, crossed her arms, and said, "Okay. Sing us your 'awesome' song that you wrote in five minutes, Capri."

Capri started playing a fast, happy-sounding melody on the piano and sang:

"I wanna tell you something,

That everyone should know,

About a place that you all know—"

Annie interrupted. "Capri, you can't rhyme 'know' with 'know,' they're the same word."

Capri ignored her and kept singing:

"Hey everybody, listen to me:

Do you like math and his-to-ry?

English? Science? Art and PE?

Well, there's an awesome place, for you and me!"

Annie rolled her eyes.

"You can walk to it or take the bus,

It's a place made just for us!"

Annie did a big yawn.

"Five days a week, we do something cool,

We get up in the morning and we go to school!

Our teachers are awesome, smart, and fun,

And the snack lady makes a great Morning Bun!"

Zeke, who was snapping his fingers to the beat, said, "I love those Morning Buns!"

I have to admit, they are pretty great.

"School is cool! Say it with me!

School is cool! Sing along with Capri!"

Annie stood up and yelled, "STOP!"

Capri stopped, though you could tell she didn't want to.

"I didn't get to do my drum solo!" complained Dog Hots.

"I am never, ever singing that," said Annie.

Capri smiled. "You don't have to. I will."

"I'm the best singer!" said Annie.

"Tom is the best singer!" said Capri.

She had a point.

"That is the worst song ever written," said Annie.

That wasn't true. Annie had never heard "I Love My Little Luca." It was a million times worse.

"Capri, I have a question," said Abel. "Is the song meant to be ironic? Satirical? A joke?"

"No!"

"It *is* a joke and we are not doing it!" said Annie.

Capri got up off the piano bench. "Who made you the boss of this band?"

Annie looked around at everybody. "Okay. Let's vote. Who wants to do Capri's ridiculous song?"

Capri's hand shot up and so did Dog Hots's. She turned to Zeke and said, "Zeke, you can run across the stage with a sparkler and a flashlight *and* a streamer if we do 'School Is Cool.'"

"Sorry, Annie," said Zeke, raising his hand.

"Who wants to do 'Spying'?" said Annie, as she raised her hand and looked at me and Abel.

Capri's song was dumb, but if we did it we might actually win the contest and go to Hollywood Hamburger Hang. Maren Nesmith had bragged to everybody about when she went there. She said you got to eat on sets from famous movies and they had ginormous hamburgers. I wanted to win, but I didn't want to hurt Annie's feelings. I didn't know what to do. It was a Conundrum conundrum.

Abel raised his hand to vote for Annie's song, and so did I.

"It appears we have a tie," said Abel. "Shall we flip a coin?"

"I'm not doing 'School Is Cool'!" yelled Annie.

"I'm not doing 'Spying'!" yelled back Capri.

I was getting hungry. "Can we have some nachos and then decide?"

"No!" said Annie.

Then, I got an idea. But I shouldn't have said it out loud.

"What if we do Capri's song this year and do 'Spying' next year?"

Annie erupted like a science-project baking-soda volcano.

"Forget it! I'm going to do *my* song by *myself*! I don't need you guys! You are all fired!"

The band broke up for the third time.

41.

The Bat in the Hat

I've got an excellent idea, T-Man!"

"What . . . ?" I always get a little nervous when Zeke says that.

"Let's do a magic act!"

"We're not magicians, Zeke."

"I know, but you can turn into a bat and smoke and nobody knows that. I bet we could do some awesome tricks!"

The talent show auditions were in three days and we were trying to come up with a new act. I have to admit, magic was a good idea. We looked at some videos of magicians doing tricks online. Zeke wanted to pull a bat (me) out of a hat, instead of a rabbit, but I knew we could do better tricks than that.

Eventually, we came up with a pretty good five-minute act. I thought we had a good chance of winning the night at Hollywood Hamburger Hang.

The school had to have two days of auditions because so many people wanted to be in the show, so Zeke and I didn't get to see every act that tried out. We auditioned on the second day. Principal Gonzales, Mr. Stockdale, and Ms. Heckroth were sitting in the front row of the auditorium with notebooks and pens. I checked to see if Tanner Gantt was lurking nearby with garlic. He wasn't.

We watched the other kids audition. There were rappers, piano players, singers, guitar players, lip-synchers, violinists, some bands, some skits, and dancers.

Capri rapped "School Is Cool" with Dog Hots playing drums. He did a solo in the middle of the song, and Ms. Heckroth had her fingers in her ears the whole time.

Annie sang "Spying" by herself, playing guitar. She sounded great. Now I sort of wished we'd done that song.

Abel ended up doing a juggling act. What *can't* he do?

"The next act to try out," said Ms. Heckroth, "is Zeke Zimmerman and Tom Marks."

We walked onto the stage. Zeke bowed and said, "I am The Amazing Zimmerman and this is my partner, The Mystifying Marks."

Zeke had on a tuxedo he'd worn at his sister's wedding and a top hat. I wore my suit. I felt like Abel. We used an old trunk my mom had in the attic. I got in the trunk and closed it, and Zeke waved a wand over the top.

"Oingo boingo!"

I turned into a bat and hid in a tiny corner of the trunk, under a flap that we made. The Amazing Zimmerman opened the trunk.

"He has . . . vanished!"

He closed the trunk. "And now, The Mystifying Marks will magically reappear!"

I changed back into me. Zeke opened the trunk, and there I was.

Next, I stayed on stage while Zeke went in the audience. He had Ms. Heckroth pick a playing card from a deck and show it to him. He whispered what card it was under his breath. I could easily hear him across the room.

"Is it the three of spades?" I said.

"Yes," said Ms. Heckroth. "Amazing."

"Well, I am The *Amazing* Zimmerman," said Zeke. "For our final illusion, we will need a volunteer from the audience. Principal Gonzales, will you please join us onstage!"

He came onstage and asked, "You're not going to make *me* disappear, are you?"

It wasn't a very good joke, but we laughed because he was one of the judges.

I went behind the curtain and turned into smoke. Zeke pretended to throw a smoke bomb, and the smoke (me) came out from underneath the curtain. I lifted Principal Gonzales up off the ground and floated him around. He couldn't figure out what was happening.

"What? . . . Who? . . . How?"

I put him back down, went back under the curtain, and changed back into me, and then we took our bows.

Principal Gonzales quietly asked, "Are you using any Vam-Wolf-Zom powers that we don't know about?"

"A magician never tells," said The Amazing Zimmerman.

The next day they put up a list of the acts for the show. Annie, Capri, Dog Hots, Abel, Zeke, and I all got in. There were some names that I didn't recognize, but I wasn't worried. Zeke and I had the greatest magic act of all time.

Who could possibly beat us?

42.

The Kid No One Had Ever Heard Of

The night of the show, Principal Gonzales was the emcee. The first ten acts were okay, but not great. Then, Annie performed about halfway through.

She sang "Spying" and got a standing ovation. As I stood there watching, I thought to myself, *Annie's going to start a new band with new people and get rich and famous someday. They'll interview me and say, "You used to be in a band with Annie Barstow, the biggest singer in the world.*

She fired you because you didn't want to do what became her number one hit song, 'Spying.' How do you feel?"

Gram once told me that the Beatles had a drummer named Pete Best, and just before they got famous, they fired him and got a *new* drummer named Ringo Starr. I bet Pete Best was really, really, really mad. That's how Zeke, Abel, Dog Hots, Capri, and I would feel someday. We were all going to be Pete Bests.

Capri and Dog Hots came on to do "School Is Cool." A lot of kids in the audience laughed and some of them booed. I was so glad we didn't do that song. Capri started crying and ran offstage, so Dog Hots did a drum solo until Principal Gonzales made him stop. The audience actually liked that part.

Principal Gonzales yelled at the audience. "If I hear one more boo, for any act, I will cancel this show . . . *right now!*"

I felt bad for Capri. When she came backstage, she threw her arms around me for some reason. I didn't know what to do. I patted her on the back three times. She stopped crying, so I guess that worked. There was a big wet spot on my shoulder. I hoped it dried by the time we went on.

"Please welcome our next act," said Principal Gonzales. "Skull Nightmare."

From the other side of the stage, Ross Bagdasarian, carrying a guitar, and Gary Nathanson, holding a pair of drumsticks, walked on-stage. They were followed by Tanner Gantt, carry-ing the beat-up, black bass guitar that I'd seen in his room. *That's* why he'd been hanging out with those guys. They must have auditioned on the first day.

Their music was loud and fast, and I had to admit it, though I didn't want to . . . they were pretty good. Maybe even better than pretty good. The audience went crazy, cheering and yelling. I really wanted to hate them because of Tanner Gantt, but I couldn't because they were good. It also reminded me that Conundrum could use a bass player. Then, I remembered there was no more Conundrum.

Zeke and I were the next act. Tanner Gantt sneered as he walked by us. "Beat that, magic boys."

"And now we have a magic act," said Principal Gonzales. "The Amazing Marks and The Mystifying Zimmerman!" He messed up our names. It went downhill from there.

It's hard to say whose fault it was that our act was a complete disaster. I say it was Zeke's fault for getting excited and jumping up on top of the trunk, which he'd never done and I didn't know he was going to do. He says it was my fault for thinking something had gone wrong when I heard him jump on the trunk, and for coming out of my hiding place.

Anyway, the trunk tipped over and I fell out and everybody saw that I was a bat.

"It's Marks!"

"He *can* turn into a bat!"

"It's about flipping time!"

"I hope he doesn't have rabies!"

"Fly, dude!"

I flew around the stage, because I thought it might save the act. It didn't. We got disqualified because there's a rule that you can't have animals in the talent show. I guess somebody brought a dog to do tricks last year and it bit Principal Gonzales.

Now everybody knew I could turn into a bat and fly. I guess it was good to get it out in the open.

Meanwhile, the show was almost over. There was only one more act.

"Our final act is Eric Blore," said Principal Gonzales.

This kid came onstage. I'd never seen him before and neither had Zeke. There's always a kid like that at school. You've never seen them and then, all of sudden, they appear out of nowhere. He was short, sort of chubby, and wore glasses and a suit and tie. He tripped on the microphone cord when he came out, and some people laughed.

Then, he sat down at the piano and played some piece by that guy named Mozart at ninety miles an hour. Teachers *love* acts like that. I knew he'd win. You can't beat a kid who looks like that playing piano at ninety miles an hour.

Eric Blore won the trip to Hollywood Hamburger Hang.

o o o

After the show, the former members of Conundrum all ended up together backstage. We looked at each other for a few seconds. Then everybody started talking. Annie felt bad that the audience had booed Capri. Capri admitted her song was a dumb idea. Annie said "Spying" would have sounded better with the whole band. Nobody needed to say anything about Zeke and my magic act. Dog Hots was bummed he didn't get to do his whole drum solo.

Abel said, "Perhaps we should entertain the idea of a Conundrum reunion?"

"Good idea," said Annie. "Let's get back together. And stay together."

Now, none of us would be Pete Best.

o o o

Two days later, I was walking to Annie's house for a band rehearsal. I saw Annie and Capri, from a block away, sitting on her front porch. I could hear them talking. I stopped to listen because . . . well . . . it's hard to not use my super-hearing sometimes.

"Annie, do you like Tom?"

"Yeah."

"No, I mean do you *like* like him?"

"You mean like a friend? Or like him, like, *really* like him?"

"Yeah, like that."

"Why?" asked Annie.

"Well, I think he *likes me* likes me. On Christmas, he gave me some perfume called Love Dreams."

"Seriously?"

"Yeah, but it gave me a rash, so I threw it away. I didn't tell him," said Capri. "Did he give you anything?"

"He gave me a book."

"What book?

"*We Died to Fall in Love.*"

"Seriously?"

"Yeah. But it was so bad, I could barely read one chapter. I'm not going to tell him."

I am never buying either of them anything again.

That night, my dad was watching the news on TV. I usually don't pay attention, but my ears perked up when I heard the reporter say, "Billionaire Geoffrey Bucklezerg Kane's Las Vegas estate was broken into last night. Security cameras showed what appeared to be a large dog outside the compound. A butler went outside the gates to investigate, but the dog had disappeared. Police believe the thief then snuck into the house, which holds Mr. Kane's private collection of rare and infamous items. However, according to a spokesperson for Mr. Kane, nothing was stolen and the intruder left without being seen."

I knew who the unknown intruder was.

Darcourt.

He didn't take anything because what he wanted wasn't there. Did he know I still had the book? Would he come back? Why is life so complicated?

43.

At Long Last, 12

On January sixteenth, I *finally* turned twelve years old. I wish my birthday wasn't so close to Christmas. I wish it was in, like, May. But unfortunately, you don't get to choose when you're born.

It felt like I'd been stuck at eleven years old *forever*. Twelve would be my last year as a non-teenager. Mom and Dad sang "Happy Birthday" to me when I walked into the kitchen in the morning. Emma was sitting there, but she didn't sing. Mom threw a buttermilk biscuit at her head.

"Ow!" said Emma. "That hurt!"

"A biscuit cannot hurt you," said Mom. "Sing to your brother."

Emma started singing off-key, on purpose, until Mom jabbed her in the ribs.

Dad measured me on the doorway where we mark our heights each year. Since I was part vampire and part zombie, I was worried that I wouldn't grow, and I'd look eleven and a half forever. I was glad to see I'd grown a little bit. I guess because I was one-third werewolf I'd get taller and look older. That was good news.

That night, we went out to dinner at a barbecue restaurant called Leave It to Cleaver. Zeke came too. Emma didn't want to go because she says she's a vegetarian. She isn't. She took five bites of Carrot Boy's roast beef sandwich. I had three steaks, rare of course. The waitress was impressed. She'd never seen anybody my age, or any age, eat that many steaks.

Mom and Dad gave me a new pair of head-phones. Gram sent me a poster of one of our favor-ite classic horror movies called *Creature from the Black Lagoon*.

Emma stepped up her gift-giving game again and gave me a T-shirt she had made. It said VAM-PIRES DON'T SHOW UP IN PHOTOGRAPHS on it.

Zeke handed me two tickets stapled to a flyer.

"I got us tickets to the Comic-Con at the con-vention center next week, T-Man."

That was a great gift. I'd never been before.

"Em-Star, we gotta go too!" said Carrot Boy.

Would they *ever* run out of nicknames?

She made her stinky-smell face. "I am so not going to hang out with a bunch of nerd fan geeks, freaking out because they can get an autograph and take a picture with some person who played Storm Trooper Number Twenty-Seven in a Star Wars movie."

"Terrence McGrath is going to be there," I said, reading the flyer.

Emma grabbed the flyer and screamed. "Oh my God! Are you kidding me?!"

Terrence McGrath was this actor Emma fell in love with last year. She named her pet mouse af-ter him. The same mouse I ate and then threw up.

Terrence—the mouse, not the actor—survived and lives with Professor Beiersdorfer across the street.

"We are so going to that Comic-Con," said Emma.

° ° °

Carrot Boy, Emma, Zeke, and I went to the Comic-Con together. We got there late because Emma

took forever to get ready. The convention hall was
the size of two football fields. About half of the
people there were dressed up as characters. It was
sort of like Halloween without the candy.

That meant it was another chance for me to
wear a costume and makeup, so people wouldn't
recognize me. I wore my old Vincent van Gogh

costume that they wouldn't let me wear at school because I had a bloody ear bandage and they had a stupid No Blood Rule. Zeke, of course, dressed up as Randee Rabbit. Emma dressed up as some weird fairy princess. Carrot Boy dressed up as Ron Weasley. He had the perfect hair.

The different booths sold T-shirts, comics, action figures, posters, and other cool stuff. There were actors signing autographs and taking pictures with fans. A few were famous, but most weren't. There was a guy who'd played a zombie in one of Gram's favorite zombie movies, *Zombies on Parade*. It was about a high school marching band that turned into zombies and ate the football players. I bought an autographed picture for her birthday.

The line to meet Terrence McGrath and get a picture was about a mile long. Emma and Carrot Boy got in line. Zeke and I wandered around. A half-robot half-gorilla came up to us and quietly said, "Excuse me? Sorry to bother you. Are you Tom Marks, the Vam-Wolf-Zom?"

"Yeah . . ."

"I know I can't take a picture, because you don't show up, but can I get an autograph?"

FINALLY! SOMEONE WHO KNEW THE RULES OF VAMPIRES!

"Sure," I said.

"How much?" asked Robot Gorilla.

"What?"

"How much for your autograph?"

"Oh. Uh, nothing."

"Thanks, man!"

I was signing his paper, when all of a sudden Zeke started doing jumping jacks.

"T-Man! T-Man! Look!"

"What?"

"It's her!"

"Who?"

"It's . . . Vacuum Girl!"

44.

A Zillion Questions

Ilooked where Zeke was pointing, way across the hall. There was a big Vacuum Girl poster hanging behind a table. And sitting at the table, wearing her Vacuum Girl costume and typing on a phone, was Keelee Rapose, the actress who played her.

"We gotta meet her!" screamed Zeke.

I wanted to hypnotize him to calm him down, but he was already running toward the table.

"Okay," I said, trotting beside him. "Calm down. Don't go crazy. You're going to scare her."

"I've got a zillion questions I want to ask her about the movie."

The closer we got, the more Keelee didn't look like Keelee. Her hair was red, but it looked brighter and a lot redder than in the movie. We got nearer and you could tell it was a wig. Her Vacuum Girl costume didn't fit her anymore—she could've used a bigger size—and she looked like she'd spent a lot of time getting suntanned.

"She looks *awesome!*" said Zeke.

I knew he'd say something like that. I decided not to disagree with him, because we were getting close and she might hear us. Obviously she'd gotten older since the movie came out twenty-five years ago.

No one was lined up at her table. People walked by, glanced at her, and just kept on walking. It was kind of depressing. She had a sign that said I DO NOT HAVE THE VACUUM GIRL ACTION FIGURE! DO NOT ASK ME!

When we finally got to her, Zeke bowed.

"Hello, Ms. Rapose. My name's Zeke Zimmerman. I am a big fan. It is an honor to meet you. I wrote you once and asked if you'd marry me, and you sent me a picture signed 'I love you' with a heart."

"You wanna buy a picture with me, kid?" she said in a husky voice that sounded like Tanner Gantt's mom.

"Yes, please!" said Zeke.

She slowly got up from her chair, grunting a bit, and pulled out a vacuum that she'd tried to make look like the one from the movie. Zeke stood next to her, with a huge smile. I took their picture with one of those instant cameras and she signed it.

Zeke said, "Ms. Rapose, out of respect for you, I didn't buy the action figure of Vacuum Girl. It didn't look like you!"

"Of course it didn't look like me! It was a man. You should've bought one though," she growled, sitting back down. "Those are worth a fortune."

"I know. This is my best friend, Tom. He had one, but his dog ate it."

She shook her head. "I used to have ten of 'em. I gave 'em away to some kids in my neighborhood, like an idiot." She turned to me. "Do you want a picture, kid?"

"No thanks," I said.

She picked up her phone and started typing.

"Was it fun making *Vacuum Girl*?" asked Zeke.

"No," she said, not looking up from her phone.

"In that scene where you sucked Dr. Badminton into your vacuum and then he dragged you in, was that you or a stunt person?"

"I can't remember," she said, grumpily.

"Did you have a favorite scene?" asked Zeke.

"No."

I felt bad for Zeke. She was being rude.

"Did you like the actor who played Mr. Windshield Wiper?"

"No!" She finally looked up from her phone. "Hey, kid, you got your picture. We're done here."

"I just have a few more questions."

She sighed. "You think I *like* doing this? Sitting here, signing pictures of myself from when I was twenty-two, from the only movie I ever did, one of the worst movies ever made, and talking to the five or six nerds who bother to stop by and ask me stupid questions?"

"Oh. . . . I'm . . . I'm sorry . . ." said Zeke, quietly.

He looked like he was going to cry. I didn't know what to do.

Then I thought, *What would Annie do?* Zeke started to walk away, but I stopped him.

"Wait a minute, Zeke."

I turned around to Keelee.

"Excuse me," I said. "My friend was very polite to you and he bought a picture. You should be grateful he even came over to talk to you. It's not like you have a big line of people. He shouldn't be apologizing to you; *you* should be apologizing to him. You should be nice to your fans. Not rude."

It felt pretty good to say that.

For a second, Keelee looked like she might hit me with her vacuum. But instead, *she* started crying. It seems like a lot of people have been crying around me lately.

"You're . . . you're right," she said, putting her head in her hands. "I'm sorry. . . . I flew in late last night and I didn't sleep well. It's been a long day." She looked at Zeke, wiped her eyes, and smiled. "What's your name again?"

"Zeke."

"Okay, Zeke. Ask me *anything* you want."

Zeke asked her a lot of questions. Afterward, Keelee gave him a hug and a free signed poster . . . *and* . . . the apron that she wore in the movie.

Zeke started crying. "I'll keep this forever! I promise I'll NEVER sell it!"

She pointed at me. "You've got a good friend there, Zeke. You're lucky."

o o o

The Comic-Con was about to close, so we met up with Emma and Carrot Boy. She showed me the signed picture she got with Terrence. Her face looked like she was on a roller coaster.

Carrot Boy said, "Dude, she was so nervous, she was shaking like a leaf."

"No, I wasn't!" said Emma. "That stupid photographer took my bad side!"

Zeke, Carrot Boy, and I went to the restroom and left Emma staring at her picture. It was weird to be standing at the urinals next to Black Panther, SpongeBob, and a Storm Trooper. But they probably thought it was weird to be peeing next to Vincent van Gogh.

Zeke whispered, "I always wondered how Storm Troopers went to the bathroom. Now I know."

When we went back outside, Emma was talking

to a tall guy wearing a long cape. I couldn't tell from the back who he was supposed to be.

"Oh my God, you guys," Emma said. "Look who's here!"

Cape Man turned around and smiled. "Hey, Tom."

Darcourt was back.

45.

The Werewolf Returns

Hey, Lucas, good to see you," added Darcourt. Carrot Boy definitely did not think it was good to see him. He just grunted.

Darcourt put his hand out to Zeke. "I'm Darcourt. That Randee Rabbit costume is excellent!"

"I'm Zeke. Thanks. I won a prize for it."

"I am not surprised." Darcourt turned to me. "Hey, Mr. Vam-Wolf-Zom, that is one sweet van Gogh costume."

"What are you doing here?" I asked, even though

I knew. He hadn't found the book at Kane's house in Las Vegas. He knew I still had it.

"Just checking out the Comic-Con. They've got some awesome stuff here. *Rare stuff.* Like that old book that you have at your house. The one you were going to show me."

"Hey, do you want to come over?" asked Emma. "Our address is 1726 Trill Avenue."

SHUT UP, EMMA!

"Can I talk to you in private for a second?" I said to Darcourt.

We went behind a booth where a guy was selling lightsabers. Darcourt stopped smiling.

"So, Tom, it seems that Martha Livingston didn't sell that book to Mr. Kane after all."

I decided to play dumb. "She didn't? She told me she did."

"I paid a visit to Mr. Kane's place in Las Vegas. He didn't have it."

"Really? That's weird."

"It is. So, either Martha lied or you lied. Let's go back to your house, look under your bed, and find out."

WHY HADN'T I HIDDEN THE BOOK IN A NEW SECRET PLACE?!

I got an idea. I stared into his eyes.

"Darcourt . . . ?" I said, softly. "Look . . . at . . . me."

"I'm looking at you."

"Listen . . . to . . . my . . . voice. You *don't* want to see that book."

"Oh, yes I do."

"No. . . . You don't. . . . You want another book . . . called *Poems of Emily Dickinson*."

"Actually, I'm not a big fan of poetry."

"You will . . . love her book."

"Only book I want to see is *A Vampiric Education*."

"Listen to my voice. . . . No . . . you . . . don't."

"Are you trying to hypnotize me?"

"No . . . I am not. . . . But keep looking at my eyes."

"I'll cut to the chase: Let's go to your house and get the book. I've got my motorcycle outside. You can ride with me or I'll meet you there."

Hypnotism wasn't working. I had to try something else.

"Okay, the truth is I don't have the book. My mom cleaned my room and donated it to Goodwill. I didn't want to tell Martha."

He moved closer and lowered his voice. "Don't be pulling the wool over this werewolf's eyes. I know you've got the book. And I'm going to get it, whether you want me to or not."

"How? I'm not going to let you," I said, trying to sound tough.

He smiled, and then he pointed at me and started yelling.

"Hey! It's the Vam-Wolf-Zom kid! Right here! Vam-Wolf-Zom in the house! In person! Check it out! He's signing autographs! For free!"

People started running over and within seconds I was mobbed. I couldn't move. And that's when Darcourt escaped. He was fast. Really fast. *Werewolf* fast. By the time I broke free from the crowd and ran outside, I saw him speeding away on his motorcycle.

"Turn to bat, bat I shall be!"

Bam!

I changed into a bat and took off after Darcourt.

I caught up with him on the freeway. He had to be going 80 or 90 miles an hour. I was hoping he'd get pulled over for speeding. No such luck.

But I had an advantage. Darcourt had to follow roads. Bats don't. I banked off to the side and flew straight toward my house. I'd beat him easily.

I was almost home. I could see it in the distance.

And then the owl appeared.

46.

Why Did It Have to Be Him?

The owl came out of nowhere and grabbed me in his talons. It was the same owl that had tried to serve me to his kids for dinner. I guess he was my official Mortal Enemy.

After our first encounter, I looked up "owls" on the Internet. They're raptors. Their grip strength is amazing. Sometimes people have to *cut off* an owl's legs to get something out of their grip. But as strong as that grip is, they can only carry about three times their weight.

I decided to change into a human, so he'd have to drop me.

"Turn to human, human I shall be!"

The owl was surprised when the bat he was holding turned into a twelve-year-old kid. My weight started to drag him down, so he let go and I fell. As I got close to the ground I turned back into a bat, so I could land, and then turned back into me.

I was only a block from my house, running by the park, when out of the corner of my eye I saw Dennis Hannigan, The Scariest Teenager in the World. He was on the grass, sitting on some poor kid's chest with his fist raised, about to punch the kid in the face. I stopped running. The kid looked over.

It was Tanner Gantt.

He was crying. I'd never seen him do that. But I'd probably be crying too, if Dennis Hannigan was about to punch me in the face.

WHY DID THIS HAVE TO HAPPEN NOW?!

Did I save Tanner Gantt, who probably deserved to be punched, but risk Darcourt getting the book? Or did I go straight home and beat Darcourt there?

It was a conundrum.

"Where's my money, Tanner?" said Hannigan.

"I-I-I don't have it. I'll get it, I promise," he said in a high-pitched voice I'd never heard before.

"Hey!" I yelled.

Hannigan looked over at me. I was pretty far away so I don't think he knew who it was.

"Mind your own business!"

"Get off of him!"

Hannigan said about every swear word I've ever heard and a few I'd have to look up later.

"Get off of him!" I said again, louder.

"Who's gonna make me?"

"I am."

Hannigan laughed. "Who are you, kid?"

"I'm Tom Marks. The Vam-Wolf-Zom."

That information didn't seem to impress him. I was in a hurry, so I ran over, picked up Hannigan, threw him on the ground, and knelt down on top of him, like he'd done to Tanner.

"You can leave right now," I said. "Or I can rip your throat out, suck your blood, and eat your brain." I opened my mouth and bared my fangs.

Hannigan looked like he was about to wet his pants, which would've been disgusting but funny at the same time.

"You-you-you can't do that," he said, sounding just as high-pitched as Tanner Gantt had. "You'll get arrested and go to prison."

"Maybe. . . . But I haven't eaten in a while. So, I really can't control myself."

"Okay, okay!" said Hannigan. "I'll go! Let me up!"

I got up. Hannigan stood shakily and pointed at Tanner Gantt. "You're dead."

I said, "No, Hannigan. *You're* dead if you ever bother him again."

I don't know why I said that. Now I was Tanner Gantt's personal bodyguard. Hannigan walked away, got in his car—which he'd probably stolen—and drove off. Tanner Gantt got up and brushed off his pants. He didn't look at me.

"I gotta go," I said.

As I ran off, I *think* Tanner Gantt quietly mumbled, "Thanks." But I'm not one hundred percent sure.

I bet he was more embarrassed I saw him crying than the fact that I was the one who'd saved his life. Or at least saved his face from getting smashed.

As I ran to my house, I thought to myself, *Of all the lives I had to save, why did it have to be Tanner Gantt's?*

Why couldn't it have been Annie's? She might've finally written a nice song about me.

Or Olivia Dunaway's? She probably would've hugged me and maybe even given me a kiss.

Or Ms. Heckroth's, who'd say, "Thank you for saving my life, Tom. No more math homework for you for the rest of the year!"

Or Geoffrey Bucklezerg Kane's, who'd say, "Thanks, kid. Here's a million bucks!"

I got to my house, ran in the front door, raced upstairs into my bedroom, and reached under the bed.

The baseball glove was there.

The book was not.

Darcourt had gotten there first.

47.

The Quest

Martha Livingston was going to kill me.
     I started to make a list of what I could say
to her:

REASONS I DON'T HAVE A VAMPIRIC EDUCATION ANYMORE
1. I lost it. (How? Where? I never took it out of the house.)
2. A vampire showed up and I lent it to him. Her. It. (Martha probably knows

all the vampires and would ask what
their name was.)
3. My dog ate it. (A classic excuse, but
Muffin *had* eaten Vacuum Girl.)
4. It disappeared when I said some acci-
dental magic words over it. (Lame)
5. Emma found it, looked it up on the
Internet, discovered how much it was
worth, and sold it on eBay. (That could
actually have happened.)

I took off my Van Gogh costume. I was working on reason #6 when the last bat on Earth that
I wanted to see appeared on my windowsill and
tapped on the glass with her wing. *Why* was Martha here? I opened the window, and she flew in
and transformed into herself.

I tried to act super casual.

"Hey, Martha. I finally figured out how to transform into smoke. Want to see me do it?"

"All in good time. Darcourt is on his way here.
Give me the book! Quickly!"

I was going to use reason #5, but I decided to tell
her the truth. Sometimes that saves a lot of time.

Martha was strangely calm.

"I feared that would occur," she said, and started
pacing back and forth.

"What do you think he's going to do with it?"

"Share our secrets with The Council of Were-wolves, or even worse, with The Society of Shape-shifters."

"Who are they?"

"Two groups you never wish to meet. That is why you and I are going to stop him."

"*Us*? We're going to stop him? The two of us? Together?"

"That is what 'You and I' means."

"Wait—How'd you know that Darcourt was coming here?" I asked.

"There was an alert on the vampiric-dot-com website."

"What?! There's a website? You never told me about that!"

"It was just launched. I was on my way here to tell you when I chanced upon the alert."

She stopped pacing and stared at me with her amazing green eyes.

"Thomas Marks, you must join me in what will be, most certainly, highly dangerous, but possibly of historic significance."

"Um . . . I can't. I have a math test tomorrow."

"Fie on math! Fie on school! I thought you were made of stronger stuff. This is a matter of grave importance to your fellow vampires."

"What do you mean *fellow* vampires? I didn't join The Vampire Club!"

"The second you were bitten, you became part of an ancient community, whether you desired it or not."

"Well, I didn't! And I'm not going to do it."

All of a sudden her eyes looked even greener than before. Was she trying to hypnotize me? I looked away.

She lowered her voice. "Then do it for me. Or do it for yourself. For your very life may depend upon it."

My *life*? That was sort of a game changer.

"Okay . . . I'll go. How do we find out where Darcourt went?"

"Use your wolf sense of smell. His scent should be strong."

I sniffed the inside of my baseball glove. Mostly leather, but I could smell the book and Darcourt's scent too.

"I can smell him."

"Good. We may be flying a great distance. Do you need to attend to any personal matters before we depart?"

"What do you mean?"

She sighed. "Do you have to go to the bathroom?"

"No."

We changed into bats and flew to the windowsill.

I looked around the night sky. "We've gotta be really careful, there's an owl out there somewhere."

Martha grinned. "There is always an owl . . . somewhere."

Off she flew, and I followed.

We flew pretty low, so I could follow the scent.
We traced it to the highway. He was heading north.

"The scent is getting stronger," I said.

"Good news indeed. We are getting close."

"What're we going to do when we find him?"

"Demand he turn over the book."

"And what if he says 'no'?"

"Then, we shall take it back by force."

"Do you think he'll fight back?"

"You may count on it."

"Um. . . . Can the two of us beat him?"

"I could likely subdue him on my own. . . . But the combined power of a vampire *and* a Vam-Wolf-Zom guarantees it."

I was glad she was confident.

I wasn't.

We kept flying above the highway, looking down at the cars and trucks speeding along. We saw a line of trucks and trailers going in the opposite direction, carrying carnival rides: a Ferris wheel, Gravitron, and a Tilt-A-Whirl. I saw the Deep Fried Cheeseburger Donut trailer go by and started to get hungry.

"There he is!" shouted Martha Livingston.

We saw Darcourt's motorcycle in the distance.

And then something else caught my eye. A smaller truck, part of the carnival convoy, towing a trailer with a sign on the side.

> *100% REAL. WHAT IS IT?*
>
> *MAN OR MONSTER?*
>
> *SEE THE ZOMBIE IF YOU DARE!*

"Martha! I gotta go!"

"I told you to go before we departed!"

"Not that! I gotta get to that trailer that just passed us! The zombie that bit me is in there!"

"How can you be certain?"

"It's the same exact sign!"

She looked over as we flew side by side.

"That zombie is no concern of ours at this moment."

"But I have to go see it!"

"No, you do not! The fate of the vampire world may be in our hands. We must get the book from Darcourt."

"But I don't know where the zombie's going. I may never find it again. This may be my one and only chance. Zombies don't have very long life spans!"

"And what on earth will you do? Have a pleasant conversation? Zombies do not speak."

"*I* do!"

"You are not a typical zombie."

"You haven't met every zombie in the world. Some talk in the movies." I looked behind me and saw the zombie trailer disappearing. "I met the vampire and werewolf that bit me. I need to meet the zombie. And you said you could take Darcourt by yourself."

"I may have, perhaps, exaggerated my abilities."

"I gotta see that zombie!"

"If you go, Thomas Marks, I shall never forgive you!"

The longer we argued, the farther away the zombie was getting.

"I'm sorry, Martha, I have to. I'll catch up with you later. Or I'll find you on vampiric-dot-com. I promise!"

She said an expression I had never heard her say before.

I banked to the right, away from Martha, beating my wings as fast as I could. Eventually, I caught up to the zombie trailer. I flew down and landed on top of the trailer, hanging on with the claws on my feet. (They're claws. I finally looked it up.)

How to get inside?

I looked for a small opening or crack to slide through on the roof, but there was nothing. The only entrance was the door on the side, which was shut tight and padlocked with a chain. Whoever was driving the truck didn't want people getting in . . . or the zombie getting out.

How to get inside?

Duh.

My new skill.

I transformed into smoke. I almost got blown off

the trailer by the wind, but I slid over the side and in through the tiny keyhole on the door.

It was dark. "Turn to human, human I shall be." I transformed back into me. There was a pull light on a string in the middle of the ceiling. I pulled it on.

There was the zombie, tied up in a chair. Just like the first time I saw it. I moved closer. It slowly raised its head, opened its one good eye, and looked at me. It opened its mouth. Did it want to eat me? I'd never seen a zombie eat another zombie in a movie. But this was a *real* zombie. It closed its mouth. I think it knew I was one-third zombie and wasn't interested in eating me. It made some low, heavy breathing noises.

"Hello . . . .?" I said.

It stared at me.

"Do you remember me?"

It kept staring.

"You bit me. . . . About four months ago. . . . In a trailer at a gas station."

The zombie slowly nodded its head.

And smiled.

And spoke.

"Hullo . . ."

Acknowledgments

Sally Morgridge, my editor, for her excellent ideas, suggestions, and comments; and if it wasn't for her this book series might not even exist.

Bram Stoker for writing *Dracula*.

Curt Siodmak for writing the screenplay of *The Wolfman* (1941).

George Romero for writing and directing *Night of the Living Dead*.

Dr. Reiter and Dr. Marks for taking good care of me.

Mark Fearing for his nifty illustrations.

Jud Laghi, my agent, for all that important business stuff.

Cheryl Lew, Emily Mannon, Michelle Montague, and the rest of the gang at Holiday House who do a ton of work to get these books out into the world.

John Simko, eagle-eyed copyeditor, who fixes my bonehead mistakes.

Beverly Cleary for writing the first book I fell in love with, *Henry Huggins*.

Dashiell Hammett and Raymond Chandler for writing great, inspirational detective novels.

Roberta Lubick, my middle-school English teacher, who encouraged me to write.